BLOOD BY MIDNIGHT

DARK INK TATTOO
BOOK THREE

CASSIE ALEXANDER

INTRODUCTION &
CHARACTER ART

Angela: *Run.* I need to run. My boyfriend, Mark, thinks his mafia connections will be able to kill my ex. But Gray's an alpha werewolf and the leader of the Pack, Vegas's most notorious motorcycle gang. It will take more than just a mobbed up human to take him down. To protect my boyfriend and my son—we have to run.

Jack: I'm the only one strong enough to save Angela—but even I can't take on an entire werewolf gang. Which means I have to talk to Rosalie: the vampire who made me, the Mistress I despise. If I don't, Angela and her son are as good as dead—so I'll do it, even if swearing allegiance to Rosalie kills me. Again.

She's a werewolf in danger.
He's a vampire about to sell his soul.

Welcome to Dark Ink Tattoo, where needles aren't the only things that bite...

Dark Ink Tattoo is a scorching paranormal in the vein of Sons of Anarchy, with strong sexual situations and bisexual MCs.

Content warnings can be found on cassiealexander.com.

CHAPTER ONE
JACK

I woke up in my own bed, having left Fran's an hour before dawn. Fran was right, Rosalie was the only tie I had to the rest of Vegas's supernatural community, but I was supremely reluctant to call on her. Any time I reminded her I existed she reminded me of the debt I owed her, and if she ever bothered to ask me about Tamo... even though years had passed since his death, discovery still felt like a matter of time. I had no doubt her anger would still be fresh, no matter how long it'd been, even if she didn't find out for a century.

I fed Sugar, took a shower, and did anything else I could think of to do before heading over to Vermillion around eleven.

DUE TO THE circumstances surrounding my creation, I avoided Vermillion as much as possible, a détente that I think both Rosalie and I enjoyed. I was never sure what I was to her—each time I arrived she treated me like a prodigal son, but seemed content to lose track of me for months at a time. Since she always knew where I was,

I knew the freedom I felt was just an illusion, but one that I was glad she seemed careful not to break.

The music was as loud as ever but the place had undergone a remodel—it was shining and clean and lacked the air of desperation that could so quickly perfuse these kinds of places, though I wouldn't put it past Rosalie to mesmerize the last of her patrons every night, turn the lights on, and make them polish tables and sweep floors like some kind of enchanted stripper-loving zombies.

"Jack?" she asked from behind me, a question even though she had to know who I was.

I braced myself, readying an obedient smile before I even turned. "Rosalie."

Her eyes traveled my face, trying to discern the reason I was there. "It's been so long—to what do I owe the pleasure?"

"I have a few questions for you."

One of her perfect eyebrows quirked. "Really? That sounds like you need my help. Can it be?"

My teeth grit shut. It would be putting myself further in debt to her and both of us knew it. So far, I'd been 'working' off my debt by doing occasional jobs for her—because if I didn't, she'd make me. A conquering smile spread across her face, lighting up her dark brown eyes, making her lift her head in triumph, revealing the neck I wanted to bite and then strangle.

"Yes."

She lowered her head again to stare at me. "How badly? I want to hear it in your voice."

"Bad enough that I'm here," I said, flatly.

"True!" she exclaimed, glorying in her power. A girl ran up to her and started talking in a rushed voice while giving me nervous glances. Rosalie cut her short, gave her a brusque order, and then turned back toward me. "Well, Jack, it looks like you arrived just in time."

I didn't ask what for—she turned, and I knew I was supposed to follow.

S<small>HE LED</small> me to the back of the club, which had also been remodeled since I was there last. She pulled me through the room with all the alcoves, each facing onto its own pole, some of them occupied, while the entire group of them faced a currently lonely stage. It was impossible to walk past without remembering Thea. Rosalie looked over her shoulder at me as I slowed down without thinking.

"You're going to have to get better about forgetting the past. Forever is a very long time."

"Have you forgotten everyone you've lost?" I asked before thinking where it could lead.

"I've even forgotten how many I've lost," she said.

"Is that true?"

I could see her considering lying, before deciding not to. "No. But it sounds nice, doesn't it?"

I reluctantly nodded. I didn't want to forget Thea, or anyone else that I'd lost—if I could, I wouldn't be here, waiting to ask her questions about The Pack for Bella. But what would happen when I outlived Paco and everyone else I knew? All the more reason I should be on my own.

We arrived in front of a closed door, although music thumped behind it like a secret heart, and Rosalie fully turned.

"I've got a group of women in and they're getting rowdy—too timid to go watch boys, too hetero as a group to enjoy women. They think they're being risqué, but they were killing the rest of the club's mood, so I threw them in here." She gave the door a dark glance. "I need them to either drink until they're fun or I need to throw them a bone. Yours, to be particular."

"What? No—can't you whammy them?"

Her head tilted, framing her brown shoulder in black curls. "Is that what you call it?" She sounded amused. "Trust me, I'm more experienced at it than you. What happens if I tell them they had fun here? They come back tomorrow night, without knowing why, and don't spend any money again? Worse yet, they bring more friends?"

"So tell them to go."

"I could, but what if that creates lingering negativity that compels them to tell others they had a bad time? The First Seven never had to contend with Yelp."

I blinked. She'd never mentioned the First Seven before—I wanted to ask who they were, but who knew what that would cost me? "Then tell them they were never here at all."

"Ah, I could—but what about cab receipts, drinks charged to credit cards, and photos?" She mocked them, miming taking an imaginary selfie with one hand. "The world's a complicated place, Jack, and I have a business to run. I'd rather take care of their problem organically. With your beautiful, indefatigable, organ, to be more precise," she said, and brought her imaginary camera down to pat between my legs. I stepped back before she could touch me, and her nostrils widened at my small defiance. "You are mine, Jack. I let you forget that because I enjoy reminding you, repeatedly, but trust me that the day that I tire of you I will paint the floor with your blood."

The words tripped off her tongue as she smiled and the girl from earlier ran up. She waited to be polite, thinking that she'd inter-rupted some casual conversation, and without taking her eyes off of me Rosalie put her hand out for what the girl held—a leather collar and a long matching leash. I knew it was meant for me, just as I knew I couldn't escape.

"Rosalie," I said, turning her name into a plea.

She tsked and came forward like she was about to embrace me, buckling the collar around my throat. "You've fed recently, I can tell. You'll be fine." She clasped the leash to the collar's metal buckle as I looked past her at the door. "It's not a lion's den, Jack—and you're not a Christian, besides." She made to tug at the leash and I had a split second to decide if I would obey on my terms or hers.

"And then you'll answer all my questions?" I quickly asked.

"If they leave here satisfied, yes." She turned her back on me and snapped the leash, pulling me toward the door.

I FOLLOWED her into the hidden room. It was circular, with mirrors against one wall, and Maya spun around the pole on a central stage. Five women from their late twenties to mid-thirties were chatting amongst themselves at high volume, fresh drinks in hand, empty drinks across all the tables behind them. One of them had a crown on, and a sash—only instead of being Miss Universe, it proclaimed her Bachelorette. Two of the women hovered nearer than the rest— her sisters or maid of honor or what not. They were all wearing neon glowsticks as necklaces, slouching on each other in a buzzed fashion —it was clear that Maya's presence was almost an afterthought.

But one by one, as they saw Rosalie and me, they quieted. "Maya, you're out," Rosalie said. She practically leapt from the stage and ran for the door, casting a pitying look behind.

"Aww," complained the only woman who'd been paying Maya any attention. The rest of them stared.

"Are you here to kick us out?" asked one of them, in a tone that said she was eager to complain.

"No, ladies—I've brought you an extra special treat." She wound her way through their group with me an obedient three steps behind, displaying her control over me like I was a dog at a show. When we reached the stage she gracefully stepped up and knotted the end of the leash around the pole, giving me a six foot range.

"Who is he?" asked the woman closest to the bachelorette.

"This is Jack. Jack's a friend." Rosalie said, giving my cheek a meaningful tap, before walking out and abandoning me.

I watched the wall behind the stage, my back to them, as they watched my back in silence. *Goddammit.* I never should've listened to Fran.

I braced myself and turned, ignoring the collar's chafe. "Hello ladies," I said, and hopped up to sit on the end of the stage, giving myself some slack.

"You're not her type!" one of the women exclaimed, moving herself in front of the bachelorette bodily, like a human shield.

I shrugged one shoulder. "Okay?"

The women seemed confused by this.

"What's the meaning of this?"

"Who're you?"

"Why're you here?" they asked, almost as one.

Just like in prison I heard you needed to take out or befriend the biggest asshole—in any group of women there was one whose opinion counted the most, no matter what. And tonight it was hers, the bachelorette. As long as she was having fun, no one else mattered.

I stared her down, not looking away, and for her part she didn't look away either, knowing the night was hers to decide. "I was specifically told to make sure you have a good time." I spoke only to her and ignored the others.

"We should go—"

"He's cute—"

"What would Daryl think about this?" asked the human shield, her voice booming over the others. I was guessing Daryl was the groom and that she was his sister. One of the girls in back leaned over her table, where the others couldn't see, giving me a distracting view of her cleavage. When she realized I'd noticed she grinned and leaned back, as things otherwise devolved into chaos, women debating the merits of men in general and Daryl in particular.

"Ladies!" I shouted, bringing them to order. I only had a brief window to turn this ship around and gain Rosalie's cooperation. "Let's play a game."

At that, silence ruled. "What kind of game?" Cleavage asked me.

"The only game that matters," I said, relishing both the quiet and their attention. "Truth or dare."

One of the girls sputtered her drink, but some others cheered, "Yes!" and one clapped her approval.

"You go first," I told the bachelorette.

She set her drink down slowly. I imagined her rowdier friends —*or relatives?*—had talked her into this, because she was a plain girl, the kind you could pass by every day at work and never notice. But when she smiled at me her whole face lit up and I saw what Daryl might have seen. "Truth or dare?" she asked.

"Truth," I said.

They conferred as a group, before she returned with their question. "How many girls have you slept with?"

I was a bit taken aback. "Uh—more than I can count?"

"Really?"

"Bragger."

"That's bullshit—"

"How many guys have you slept with, Susan?"

The bachelorette eyed me. "That wasn't really an answer."

"Sorry. If I could count them, I would. But let's have a redo— more truth."

She grinned and they huddled. "Okay—what's the weirdest place you've ever had sex?"

My stomach churned but I kept smiling. "Here."

"Too easy!" protested Cleavage.

"Truth or dare," I asked back before I lost them again, staring the bachelorette down.

"Dare," she said, and the room hushed. By the rules of the game I could dare her to do anything—but it was far too early for that. My eyes scanned their number and I read them, noticing those who'd taken off their rings for the night, the ones that were drinking now so they'd have excuses come dawn, the way the glowsticks gave all of them an ethereal glow in the room's dim light. My eyes narrowed and I knew what needed to happen next.

"I dare you to go flip the light switch."

The bachelorette's eyebrows rose, but Cleavage ran for the door on her behalf. As she got outside, the light snapped off—Rosalie somewhere, most likely listening in, making sure I behaved and didn't whammy them. Cleavage came back triumphant, too drunk to realize she'd done nothing, her blonde hair haloed in pink.

"Thank you," I said, rewarding her with a grin as she took a seat much nearer the stage.

"Ask me," she pleaded.

"Truth or dare," I asked.

"I dare you to touch him, Tabby!" another girl said.

"You heard him, you'll get a disease," muttered the human shield from earlier.

"Dare," she proclaimed.

"Then I dare you to come sit beside me up here."

Cleavage—aka Tabby—turned grandly and flipped her friends off before joining me, scooting close. I made sure not to scare her— and I thought I saw the bachelorette give her a jealous look.

"Truth or dare," Tabby asked the human shield.

The shield crossed her arms. "Truth."

Tabby asked the human shield, not me: "Why're you such a bitch, Pam?"

"This is a stupid game," Pam protested.

"It is not," said the bachelorette, daring Pam to challenge her authority on this night of all nights.

"Fine. I'm such a bitch because—because," she sputtered, looking for an answer.

"*Tell us*," I encouraged. Surely Rosalie couldn't mind me pressing a little, surely she wanted to turn this room over—

"Bobby's cheating on me." The words poured out of Pam's mouth, and her hands fell in fists to her side.

"What?" the bachelorette wheeled on her, full of sudden sympathy. "Oh my *God*, Pam."

"There's this girl at his work—I saw photos on his phone." A dam broke inside her, tears welled out, and the girls circled round. Even Tabby hopped off the stage to be near her. "I didn't want to say anything," she said, wiping one eye. "It's your weekend, Lori. I'm here, and I know he's home with her."

"Oh, Pam, I wouldn't have made you come if I'd known," Lori, my bachelorette, apologized.

"I'm so sorry," Tabby said.

"You all didn't know," Pam said, pulling her in for a sloppy hug. "None of you did." They were a throbbing mass of girl-power for one moment, supporting Pam and plotting Bobby's demise, and I was reminded why I loved women—on top of their beauty, they were strong. For themselves, and one another, all the time.

"Come here, Pam," I suggested gently. She rose up, eyes blinking wetly, and made her way to the stage. I patted the seat beside me. "Don't worry. I don't bite."

She sat down beside me, her purse clutched in her lap like I might steal it. I could sense her doing the internal math that kept her away from me—not just thinking that this whole thing was silly or risqué, but the knowledge that men like me didn't typically find girls like her attractive—that after you've had two kids, lose your waist and get a belly, sometimes you feel like you fade away. Her rejection of me wasn't about me—it was her rejecting all mankind, preemptively.

"You know that phrase, the best way to get over someone is to get under someone else?" I asked.

Pam nodded mutely.

"Sometimes it's true," I said, then looked over at one of the quiet girls. "Truth or dare."

She looked around, like I might've been talking to someone behind her. Then I watched her steel herself. "Dare."

I let my eyes travel, looking at each of them one by one, an interloper in their lives, a witness to their grief, a testament to their hope that one frantic party would give them memories to last a lifetime. "I dare you to take that necklace off, and throw it to the back of the room."

The women conferred amongst one another with their eyes and

then with trembling hands, Lori's quietest bridesmaid unfastened the glowstick necklace and tossed it.

"Thank you...." I told her, asking for her name.

"Jamie," she almost whispered, then turned immediately to her friend. "Truth or dare."

"Truth."

"Tell us the deal with Gabriel."

Tabby laughed and Lori made a 'ooh' sound. Even Pam chuckled. The woman—Susan, by power of deduction—groaned. "He's good for me, all right?"

Pam looked to me. "Hideously unattractive man," she clarified, for my sake.

"I heard that—and I know, I know," Susan said. "But," she stood and got into the spirit of things, likely as her third drink hit. "Ladies, he is *good* at going down."

Lori rocked back, laughing, and Tabby shouted, "I knew it!" as the others hooted.

"What? James would never go there!" Susan stood up for her new man.

"You should never waste time with a man who won't," I said, backing her.

"See?" she agreed with me. "Whereas Gabriel?" she turned to address her friends. "That man needs a snorkel."

"Good, 'cause I'm getting him one for Christmas," Jamie said, coming out of her shell now that she was in the safety of the dark. Everyone laughed, even Susan.

If this didn't count as a good time, I didn't know what would. And yet: "Truth or dare," I announced to the group at large.

"Dare," Tabby shouted back.

"I dare you to take off your necklace, too."

Tabby gave me a mischievous look, and then whipped it off like it was a belt and chucked it behind her. "Truth or dare," she asked back. "Pick dare."

"Dare it is," I said.

"I dare you to kiss Pam."

I felt Pam stiffen beside me. "Oh no," she said, scooting away bodily.

"I would never do anything that someone was uncomfortable with," I said, and saw her shoulders slightly slump. She didn't want me to do anything—but she didn't *not* want me to do anything, either. "You let me know if that changes, though," I told her, with eyes full of intent. Blood rushed all over her body, distracting both of us for different reasons.

We were down to three glowsticks worth of light, and the girls had come back from too drunk, to just drunk enough.

"You told me earlier that I wasn't her type," I told Pam, with a nod to Lori. "So if I'm not, who is?"

"Daryl," Lori said with a grin.

"Daryl. Daryl's so this, and Daryl's so that," Tabby said in a sing-song, coming up to sit on my other side. "I mean, the man could probably pick up a truck, yes. But there's more to life than that."

"Like what?" I asked her.

"I dunno. Music? Poetry?"

"Head!" shouted Susan, and everyone giggled.

While I laughed along with the women, Tabby wriggled her hand in between us, and started tugging at the outer seam of my jeans. "Where's the Velcro? Why won't your pants come off?"

"Oh, they do. Believe me. Is that what you want?" I moved to stand up, leaning against the pole behind me.

"It's too dark to see," Jamie complained.

"I don't know about that. I can see you all just fine—and I think it's time for the last truth or dare." I knew more than enough about them now to give anyone who was interested a good time, person-ally. "Is the truth that you want me to get the lights turned on again? Or do some of you want to dare to see what we can do in the dark?"

The moment froze, as each of them considered what that might mean. Then Lori grinned wickedly and reached for her necklace. "I have to stay true to Daryl, ladies. But far be it from me to stand in anyone else's way of a good time." She popped the clasp of her glow-stick off, and chucked it to the back of the room. Susan looked from side to side, and took hers off, swinging it overhead like a lasso with a *whoop!* before throwing it.

Which left Pam. I turned toward her and gave her a warm smile. "Yes, no, maybe so?"

She swallowed audibly, but then decided, yanking her necklace off with force and hurling it to the back of the room, leaving me and the women in darkness.

"What now?" Tabby asked from the front of the stage.

"Now, this," I said, reaching for my phone. I turned the flashlight on and brought it up to make my face look spooky. I made a ghost noise and they laughed. "So—on our continuing journey through what I always assumed women's slumber parties to be—get those tables out of the way—set them against the back walls, please." My phone put out just enough light that all the women could partici-pate, setting all the tables and chairs back. "Good." I reached up and undid the metal clasp that kept me fastened to the leash, leaving the collar on. I stepped forward and leapt off the stage into the center of the clearing they'd provided, and they gasped, like I was a figure in a painting come off the wall.

"Seven minutes in heaven," I said, and set a recurring alarm on my phone. I whipped out a chain of five condoms, one for each of them. "I did warn you all I was a man-whore," I said and made a show of tearing them apart to hold in my bowled palms, feeling like some sort of sex magician. Things would've been easier if they were heteroflexible, but since they likely weren't, this was the next best thing.

"I'm going to turn off the light—and then each of you will have thirty seconds to find somewhere to hide from me—if you want to—or someplace to set up shop. After that, I'll find you, one by one, and offer you a condom. If you're not interested don't take one. If you are —I'm yours until the alarm."

I could practically hear their heads swivel as I laid out my terms, looking at each other, being scared to take me up on my offer and also scared to deny themselves—or others!—it.

"After everyone's seven minutes are up, Vegas rules apply."

"What're those?" Lori asked.

"The usual—what happens here stays here and all." I rested my thumb over the button to turn the light off. "Does that sound fun?"

"Sex with a stranger hide-and-seek, oh yeah, totally do that all the time," Pam said dourly.

Tabby laughed and turned towards me. "Start counting."

CHAPTER TWO
JACK

I let the light click off and started counting aloud, slowly. I heard the women run around, bumping into each other with giggles, "No, I'm here!" and "Go over there!" and "Stay beside me in case he's insane," each with easily identifiable voices. By the time I got to the twenties they'd settled themselves, but I counted more slowly because I could, drawing the moment out, feeling the unspoken tension in the air.

"The clock's ticking, ladies," I said after I reached one, and turned the volume on my phone up so everyone could hear it counting down.

The first one I sought out was Tabby. I knew from her flashing her breasts earlier she was looking for a good time—and after she'd called out Pam, she was likely unafraid of being known for it. I wanted to use her directness to break the ice.

I didn't have to go far—she'd actually scooted toward me on the stage, sitting on the edge of it while I stood just in front of her on the ground, her closed knees even with the middle of my thighs. I put a hand out for hers, found it, and offered her two condoms, making sure she felt both of them—and she understood. Even if we used

14

one, she'd still have another one to use to protest her innocence. I heard her chuckle under her breath, and then felt her knees spread as she grabbed at my belt to pull me near, then began unbuckling it quickly. I waited, tense, to see how she wanted to use me, ready to be of as much service as she required.

When my fly was undone her hand sank into my jeans like a pro, and she found me hard. She made an agreeable sound at that and wrapped her legs around my knees and calves, bringing my body close enough to feel her breath.

Then, she reached her hands up, and shucked off her shirt and bra—I knew because right afterwards, she bent over me, pressing her exquisite breasts on either side of my erection. I thrust without meaning to and stopped, but then felt her rock against me and knew that this was what she wanted. I rose up on my toes, stroking against her, feeling the silky smoothness of her skin as she made the perfect tunnel for me to stroke through. I held her shoulders to help brace myself, stroked more firmly, and in response she lowered her head so that her breath brushed the head of my cock each time it emerged, as if to taunt me. I groaned at this, and heard a questioning sound ripple through the rest of the women as they wondered just what was going on.

The clock ticked down behind us, as if keeping time for my strokes. Was this all she wanted? I could feel her blood racing with my other-sight—I knew it couldn't be. But if I misjudged her, the night was lost, and Rosalie wouldn't answer a thing.

I had to carefully dare. I pulled my hands off her shoulders and down the forward slope of her held breasts until I met her hands there and went past them to circle her nipples. I felt her thighs squeeze me in surprise, but also saw the quick wick of heat lightning in her hips as her blood sank in an instant.

I brought my fingers up to lick, one hand at a time, and returned them, finding her nipples hard. She made a soft whimper as I reached below them for their underbelly, to stroke soft fingers up, and suddenly I wondered if she was one of *those* women, the kind for whom their breasts were everything, able to come hard just from touch alone if you could stroke their nipples perfectly, like their areolas were the locks to twin safes.

When I reached her nipples again I gently pinched them to find out, and she moaned.

It would be so much easier if I could just ask her what she wanted, but it seemed like talking would break the communal spell —so instead I took control of her breasts over from her, pressing my hands against her hands until she ceded them, rubbing against her nipples with my thumbs as I kept thrusting and—I heard her hands find the condom in her lap and open it up.

What now, where now—and how much time was left? She pulled back and I let her breasts go as she found my cock with the condom, taking a moment to swirl the precum there with a fingertip, making all the nerves there ignite. I rose up on my toes for her as she grabbed for my hips and pulled me up and back until I'd clambered on the stage with her, over her, straddling her with my knees, following the intent of her hands as she pulled me higher, until I was over her chest and her breasts surrounded me again. I rocked forward and groaned and felt her shudder with delight at her control over me—but this was too much me, and not enough her.

"I'm sorry—I need too," I whispered, taking control of myself back and crawling back to lay alongside her to kiss her breasts, like she'd given me no other option. One of her hands curled in my hair and I went where it pushed me. All breasts are perfect in the dark, but hers had been perfect beforehand—and it was nothing to ignore myself and concentrate all my attention on them, kissing and caress-ing, nibbling and sucking, listening to her body and her breath, watching her blood almost boil as I tried to find the right combina-tion. Her body thrashed appreciatively as she moaned and I slid a knee up between her legs for her to rock on as her hand left my hand and found my condomed cock and stroked and—

There. It was there. I pinched one nipple and sucked the other and felt her hips flutter as her thighs squeezed my leg tight and her hand around my cock pulled the condom clean off.

She came in a series of high pitched gasps, obviously holding back screams, rocking against me as I followed her every movement with my mouth, as if I could suck the life out of her, tempted, *so tempted*, to bite.

She relaxed onto the stage floor like a rag doll, breathing hoarsely, then and only then remembering my cock. She reached for it and began to apologize. "I'm," she started to apologize, but I pressed a finger to her lips.

"Shh." My fangs were throbbing to come down, but she'd fed me well enough.

The bell rang and it was time to move on.

CHAPTER THREE
JACK

I set my cock back inside my jeans, fastened them and my belt, and then went to the next woman—Susan, sitting on a table off to the side. What had she heard and what would she think? I approached her, offering two condoms, same as I had for Tabby. She took both of them and put them down. Did she want to wait out all seven minutes, and make the other women think she'd done something she hadn't? Or had she not quite made up her mind?

My phone counted down the seconds as I wondered what, if anything, I should do—and then I saw one of her hands rise in the dark. I stepped closer so it could find me.

She was tentative, but when one of her hands reached me, she let the other one follow, until both were on my chest, still heaving from my time with Tabby. And then slowly—so slowly I knew she had to be teasing me, intentionally, they rose up until they reached the edge of my collar and grabbed hold.

I made a low and appreciative sound without thinking as she pulled me toward her—and then pushed me down, down, down, until I was kneeling. With the assurance of someone who'd done this before, she put one leg on each of my shoulders and leaned back.

She had been wearing a skirt. I cupped her ass and brought it to the edge of the table for me. Her skirt skidded higher, until the only thing between her pussy and my mouth was a thin satin strip. I went in and kissed on top of that—pushing my tongue against her clit, against the sheer fabric. In response, her legs opened wider, her ass clenched to rise up, and one hand went into my hair and *pulled.*

I started eating her out, letting the fabric shield her from me, knowing that when she'd had enough with subtlety she'd move it. I ground my chin into her pussy and felt her clit wobble as my tongue rubbed back and forth, her breath catching with each new stroke. My cock was aching and it was torturous—I knew how wet she was, if only she wanted me.

But she didn't—or rather, not that part of me. Her ass rocked her up and down as her hips fucked my face, and finally at long last she reached down with her free hand to pull her underwear aside—I growled and worked her clit as I'd worked Tabby's breasts, rubbing, grinding, sucking, rolling her clit across my tongue and back again. Whoever Gabriel was, I wanted to ruin her for him.

Her hips started to quiver, her legs tensed on my shoulders, stiffening, her thighs squeezing my head as her insistent hands pulled on my hair, hard, and—

She came with a quiet series of hisses, shuddering in front of me, as my mouth followed her to suck in every drop of life she released.

I rocked back and cleaned my mouth and chin off on my arm, just as the timer beeped.

CHAPTER FOUR
JACK

Jamie was the next woman on my clockwise rotation through the room, sitting on a nearby chair. I gave her the option of two condoms, and she snatched both of them up eagerly, tearing a wrapper open. There was a tension coming off of her, a sudden wave of urgency—and I dared to start unfastening my belt at once. Her hands found mine and urged me faster, making me push my jeans down, reaching for my cock, and expertly sliding the condom on. She grabbed my cock and steered it for me, standing herself and turning around—I didn't know where she was taking me, but after Tabby and Susan I wanted it—and I felt her whip the chair she'd been sitting in around.

The chairs were cushioned things, with an elaborate curve at the back to seem all the classier—Jamie'd realized she was the perfect height to fit herself and bent over, at the same time she pulled my cock toward her pussy.

I pulled back at the last second, afraid that we were moving too fast—but then I realized that's what she wanted—the anonymity of a brutal lay.

It was always the quiet girls you had to watch out for.

I pushed myself in and felt her give for me, all of her tight pussy opening, and it was hard not to growl my triumph, after so many other activities tonight. She was wet—I bet she'd been touching herself for, oh, fourteen minutes now, and if it was a hard fast fuck she wanted, then I was the man to give it to her.

I started plowing, in and out, using the back of the chair to pull her towards me. She was limp over it, giving into whatever fantasies she dreamed. Then her hands found purchase on the seat of the chair and she started arching back and my cock was pressing so deep inside her, I could feel all of her, each time I ground in and up and—I grabbed her ass, holding onto the beautiful flesh of it, making us both sway. I kept up in even strokes, fucking her to the sound of the ticking clock, my hips a metronome.

She started to pant, I could tell she was trying to keep telling noises down, only allowing expression through breathing—but what breaths! They started running in sync with my thrusts, and then went uneven, charging like a freight train, I was worried she'd go light headed and then pass out—but she leaned back so hard to take me and her knees started to shake. If I'd known her, I'd have wrapped my hand in her hair and pulled, or slapped her hard on her ass once to knock the orgasm out of her, or told her to come with her name, but under the current circumstances, none of that was allowed, and so I had to wait and pray—and speed up—until my thrusts were as wild as her breathing, both of us lost in the moment, grasping for pleasure.

And then it hit like lightning. She buckled, toes almost off the ground, and I felt her pussy quiver and shake and then grab, hard. I pulled her hips to me and lost myself in her, feeling my own balls pulse and cum jet.

I spent a long panting moment there, reeling from my orgasm and her strong wave of life, until the bell rang and I had to move on.

CHAPTER FIVE

JACK

The bachelorette herself was next. She was sitting on another chair—this one lower to the ground, and far more sturdy, her knees together, her hands primly in her lap. I sat down beside her and offered her both condoms, pressing them into her hands like she was Helen Keller—I didn't think she'd take me up on my offer, but I wanted her to have the same chance. After that, I prepared to sit quietly beside her until the clock ran out—except....

One of her hands rose and found my face, pressing against my lips for utter silence. I nodded into her hand, understanding. The other girls could go home with stories—but absolutely no one could know if anything happened here tonight to her. Then her hands found one of mine and brought it up, underneath her skirt.

It was a testament to her bravery—or my temptation—that she was willing to risk getting caught. With that thought in mind, I shifted the cotton of her underwear over and stroked against her folds.

Her thighs squeezed—and her hands pulled me in, begging me to feel where she was hottest.

I dared to push a finger in, feeling the walls of her pussy give way as she leaned back. Her other hand reached out for my head and caught it, bringing me down to kiss her quietly. I didn't know if this was all she wanted—but I did know that the best gift that I could give her, on her last likely night of freedom, was an orgasm.

I pushed two fingers inside her and kept stroking her clit with my thumb. Her hips rocked up and down, forcing my fingers to thrust, until she seemed to come to a decision. She pulled my hand away, and I thought the gig was up—when she handed me an extra condom.

As a vampire, I can do all sorts of things quietly that normal people cannot—open belts, open flys, and open wrappers. When I was ready for her I reached out for her hand and brought it to myself, so she could stroke me and know.

Instead, she held on, and rose to lasso one leg over my lap then the other, bracing herself on the chair back behind me. Slowly—I knew it was slow because I could hear the seconds count down—she stirred my cock into her, spinning her hips like a merry-go-round, letting my cock feel each of her walls in turn.

Any time a woman took me like this, I couldn't help but think of Thea. My jaw dropped, with sensations and with memories. Even though we had to be quiet, I wanted her to know how I felt—I rested my head against her chest and held her close as she slid down.

She cradled my head to her chest with one hand as we sealed, her hips atop my own, and then I licked my thumb and reached in to rub her.

She didn't rise and fall and I didn't thrust, those things would've made too much sound—all she did was rock on top of me as my thumb followed her clit. Her hips rolled in wide circles, swirling me into her tightness, and I knew this was her signature move, likely what Daryl lived for, and I made a mental note to be jealous on principle of men named Daryl for the rest of my too long life.

Her hand sank down to take over from my thumb and I knew the friction between us was growing, could see the way her blood flowed low, and almost feel her pussy beginning to throb—and there it was

—she spasmed around my cock, pulsing hard. Then she leaned forward and bit my shoulder, through my clothing, but nonetheless my body wanted to respond in kind—the only thing that saved both of us was the perfect wave of pleasure emanating out from her, and the closeness of my own orgasm. I cupped her head to my neck, urging her to bite me again, as my other arm wrapped around her waist and pulled her onto me, hard, and she bit down again just like I wanted her to. The pain, the shock, the beauty, the temptation—my cock stiffened inside her, pumping out its load, and I only managed silence by gritting my teeth.

We both sat there for a second, spent. Then just as carefully as she'd mounted me, she dismounted. I stroked one hand down her satin sash, likely painting myself with glitter, and then stood. I only had enough time to gather myself up before the alarm rang.

CHAPTER SIX
JACK

P am was last. I wondered if that was good or bad—she wasn't hiding, she was sitting on another one of the sturdy chairs. I announced myself on the way over to her with a slight masculine growl—and drew up short as I realized she'd been crying.

She hadn't said anything about it to the other girls. Taking another one for the team? Or wanting to be alone in her grief? I sat beside her gingerly—and instead of offering her a condom, I offered her my hand. She found it and clasped it tightly. I set the condom aside, and used my other hand to carefully find her cheek and jaw, and then stroked away the tears from her eyes with my fingertips, so she'd know that I knew what she was up to.

She took a deep breath at this, and then fell into my shoulder with muffled sobbing. I wrapped my arms around her and rocked her slowly, back and forth, brushing her hair back to chastely kiss her forehead.

I couldn't be a hundred percent sure what she was crying for— but I could guess. The loss of her life with Bobby, the fear of starting anew, not knowing who she was anymore all the way. I knew from personal experience that a great loss takes that from you, your sense of self, leaving you feeling small and adrift in a stormy ocean without a shore. I pulled her tighter to me and then kissed her forehead again.

This time, she stiffened. I was worried I'd gone too far—I sat perfectly still. But then her head reached up, and kissed the bottom of my chin.

I tilted my head so her mouth could find mine, and felt her sweet lips part to let my tongue in. I wanted to protect her from everything yet to come—I wanted her to have something to hold onto when the seas got rough—I offered her the condom again and—this time she held it. I took it back from her, knowing exactly what she needed to have next.

I undid my belt and fly, slid the condom home on my already hard cock, and picked her up like I was carrying her over a threshold. She squeaked in surprise, but didn't fight me. I cradled her to my chest, kissing her, rocking her up and down, back and forth—and then she realized what I wanted to give her, if she'd have me.

She wriggled her skirt up and reached down behind her to pull her panties aside, and with my great strength I tilted her body in just the right way so that my cock slid in between her generous thighs for its first push into her pussy.

She gasped and threw her arms around my neck as I entered her, cradling her against me, and I wondered how long that Bobby had had her, all to himself, what kind of emotional wreckage my cock would be sweeping away. I lowered her all the way down, thrusting up, and felt her squirm in delight. "Yes," she whispered, just a breath.

"Yes," I whispered back, and then sucked on her ear and felt her shiver.

We rocked there, her letting me play her up and down, my ass thrusting both of us up when I brought her low, my arms pulling her almost off of me before sliding her back down. The clock ticked down, buzzed, and none of the other women said a word or moved—clearly able to hear the sounds of us still fucking.

I started to go faster, now lowering her as I thrust up, making her take me deep, and she had a hand between her thighs, as I kissed her neck, hunching us both over.

Her breath caught, her legs kicked, and I felt her body fight me as it tried to straighten—I could tell that the life she was going to give me would be the richest one yet, thick and deep, by the way she tried to hold onto it, to taste all of it for herself before she let it leave her.

And then a wave wracked her body, and another, and a third. She was rolling against me in my arms, her pussy sucking me deep as I settled into it and let it milk me, the force of her orgasm *making* me come. I shamelessly made guttural sounds, pounding it into her, knowing she needed to feel taken, and when we were through I rocked back, still holding her to my chest.

We were silent and panting together for a long moment, when from across the room an unknown pair of hands clapped in applause.

I held Pam longer, feeling her breathe as roughly as I did, until she moved a little and I knew it was time to let her go. I carefully set her down and stood. "How about another seven minutes to move around the cabin? Straighten yourselves out, walk around some, gain plausible deniability and all that?"

"Why would anyone want to deny that?" came Tabby's voice from up on the stage, and was met with a few snickers. I hopped up behind her and clasped my collar back to the leash. Like clockwork seven minutes later—so I *knew* Rosalie was watching—the lights came back on. By then all the girls had rearranged their clothing and hair and looked like they could've just arrived out of the back of some Uber.

"Did you all have a good time?" I asked their number. From the secret smiles to the open ones, I knew they had. "Good. But now I need to ask a favor." I sat on my heels in front of them.

"Here it comes—the part where he charges us," Pam said. Earlier Pam would've been sarcastically frowning—but now she was ready to laugh. She had something up on Bobby now, and if I had have asked, she would've willingly paid.

"Nope. All you have to do is never, ever, tell anyone else about this experience. Each other, that's up to you. But I don't want to be chained up here every night." As I said the words lightly, I realized it was all too possible that they could be real. If Rosalie compelled me to do something for her, I would have to. "I want you to consider this a personal favor. From me, to all of you." I put my hand to my chest and I meant it. "And especially in honor of Lori, the luckiest bachelorette to have such true friends."

Lori held the extra condom I'd given her up. "The things I do for you ladies."

"Hey now," Susan said, showing both of hers.

Pam laughed and held hers high. Tabby giggled and threw hers to land on my feet on stage, and Jamie suggestively tucked hers into her bra for me, in the back, where no one could see her do it.

"Thank you. It's been a pleasure, honestly." I grinned at them and sat down like I had originally, legs hanging off the edge.

"The pleasure was all ours. Clearly," Lori said, looking around— then she grabbed Susan's hand and ran laughing for the door.

They all ran out in a cluster, except for Pam who lagged a little behind with a questioning look. "How...did you? And—so many times?"

"Eternal youth?" I tried, and when she didn't buy that, "Viagra?"

Her head tilted as she tried to buy that—she had to, there was no other answer that made sense. "You, sir, are a machine—and a marvel."

I smiled again at her, just for her. "My name's Jack," I said.

"Bye, Jack," she said, and ran off to rejoin her friends.

I counted to five and unclipped myself from the leash. After that performance, Rosalie had better have answers for me.

CHAPTER SIX

I WALKED BACK out into Vermillion proper, unwittingly a walking advertisement for the place, smelling of sex while wearing sprinkles of glitter. Rosalie stood behind the bar, being sultry and entertaining in turns.

"All done?" she asked after I walked up.

"Entirely," I said, unbuckling the collar and tossing it over. She caught it with one hand. If only getting rid of her control over me was as easy. I wasn't mad at the women, but this situation, where she could command me to obey—I knew what she was capable of. Sometimes the fear of it was debilitating.

"Then I think you've earned a few answers for tonight." She handed me a beer and walked to the far end of the bar, where I took the seat opposite her. I didn't like how close the other patrons were, but the thought of being alone with her was worse. "Honestly, I don't know how Olympic Gardens used to put up with this shit."

I looked from the beer to her—I knew I needed answers, but I hadn't figured out all my questions yet. I decided to start with the biggest one. "Are we alone in the world?" I asked, sounding like a man too deep in his cups.

She laughed. "I'm afraid you're going to have to be a little more specific."

I glanced at the nearest other patron, then a girl came in, striking up a conversation with his face while he started talking to her breasts, and I relaxed a little. "I fought someone recently—he wasn't one of us, but it was a close fight."

"You bit off more than you could chew?" I thought she was mocking me, but Rosalie looked concerned. I didn't like that, I didn't want her pity—and I was afraid of her fear. "What did they smell like?"

"Dog."

"Were. Which one?"

"Short, a beard. Angry."

She was leaning over now and our conversation was so quiet

29

only ones like us could hear. "Murphy. One of the Pack. You know of them?"

"Bikers."

"And werewolves. What made you try to take one on?" she asked, and then rolled her eyes before I could answer. "A woman, no doubt. You're never going to change, Jack. I swear I froze you in time."

As much as I wished that were not true.... "How do I kill one?"

"Same way as us. Silver, brute force. It's easier on a dark night—nearly impossible on a bright one—but I forbid you."

My hand squeezed the beer bottle tighter. "I didn't come here to ask permission."

"You think they won't know who hurt them? Who do you think they'll attack after that? You can go to ground—but I've built something here." She gestured to the club behind her.

"I'll kill them off one by one. I won't leave any witnesses—or survivors." Not now that I knew what they were. How had Bella gotten herself involved with werewolves?

"And what if the wolf you attacked is having a conversation similar to this with the rest of his kind right now? What did you show him of yourself?"

"No fangs, only strength."

"Nothing else about you?"

"My appearance. Same as ever."

She leaned back. "Could've been worse then. I'm not battening down the hatches for a biker war—and I don't expect to, either. You lead them to me and I let them kill you."

"Fair enough."

"Good. Other than that, do what you will." She considered me coolly. "I watched you tonight, Jack. Turning the lights off was a masterful touch, but you have to know that all my rooms like that are wired for my girls' safety. And as your Mistress, with you so near, I could hear everything—almost feel everything—through you. You could've bled any—or all—of those women in the dark, and no one would've been the wiser."

I felt fear wind in my belly and my throat squeeze. "That's not how I am."

"But you wanted to—I know it, don't try to lie."

"But I didn't."

"For now," Rosalie told me with her French accent and a wicked smile. "For now."

CHAPTER SEVEN
ANGELA

After Mark left I crawled into bed and had wild dreams—literally wild. My wolf, stalking through the forest, pebbles and leaves beneath our feet, the scent of trees, wind rippling our fur. We drank from a stream and I could taste the water's cool perfection, and then—fire, somewhere close, the scent of smoke in the air, distant heat, and the sound of spring twigs snapping as the flames made them burst. We ran as one, clambering up a rocky slope in steep jumps, until we reached a cave where there was a small white wolf pup inside. We grabbed his nape gently in our fierce jaws and started racing him out of the cavern, the fire's heat lapping at our heels, sounding more and more like the engine of a motorcycle.

"Mom! Mom!"

I sat up in bed, fully myself, slamming my wolf away into the box at the back of my mind. I leapt out of bed, grabbed my robe, and flew down the stairs to Rabbit's voice as I pulled it on.

"Rabbit?" I shouted back at him in fear. The TV was blaring, and he was sitting in front of it, way too close, holding a cereal bowl in his lap as he sat cross-legged.

"Mom!" he said, without looking away from his cartoon. "We're out of milk!"

I put my hand to the doorframe and fought to swallow down my panic.

THAT SET the tone for the rest of the day. I knew Mark was taking care of things—but when? And how? And would it even work? I watched a car pull out from my apartment's parking lot as I did, following me four car lengths back as I dropped off Rabbit and went to work— Mark's 'friend' watching me, the car was far too nice for the Pack. I parked near the back of Dark Ink's lot, and he stationed himself near the front, closer to harm's way.

Gray was on silver on the inside—but the Pack members outside of prison weren't. If they did come by, would one normal guy be able to stop them, no matter how well trained? I frowned at the man and he—whoever *he* was—nodded in curt acknowledgement. I turned and went inside.

Mattie was there, already working on a client. I went straight for my tiny office with my coffee, haunted by my fears, and sat down on my chair in the dark. My dream last night had been so real—and so freeing, just to live and run, before the fire'd come along. I'd felt so self-possessed and strong—in her world, my wolf always knew what to do. She never had any questions. She was always right.

I pulled open the desk drawer that held another vial of silver with an eyedropper. It was time, the full moon was coming, and from the dream I knew *she* wanted out—and yet half the dream we'd been running toward that pup and away from the fire, to save him. It didn't take a psychologist to make the jump from the wolf pup to Rabbit. She was part of me—and she was Rabbit's mother as much as I was. Did she want to keep him safe too? Was that her way of telling me? I didn't think my wolf could lie.

I crossed my arms in the darkness, hugging myself. "Do you understand what's going on?" I asked her. "Really?"

A rapping on the office door interrupted me. I knew it was Mattie from the way he cleared his throat before he spoke: "Hey boss—who's that weirdo in the parking lot?"

I shut the drawer, leaving the silver safe inside. I'd take my chances with *her* today—better her than the Pack. "I don't know, just ignore him," I told Mattie.

IT WAS A SLOW DAY—ALTHOUGH who knew if that was because of my worrisome guard staring everyone down. I did the lay-out line work on a dealer's arm, a series of morpho butterflies of varying sizes, from her elbow up, wrapping around in flight. It took a few tries to get the stencil just right but after that, following the outlines I'd created was easy for both of us—the pain wouldn't really kick in till I had to use a larger needle set to lay in colors. She sat like a rock and was pleased with the outline, making me help her take photos to show off later. After that, I got a walk-in who came straight up to the counter.

"Do you do cover-ups?" The woman who asked was average sized, but a little too lean, which made her look hungry. The scent of stale cigarettes wafted off of her.

"Yeah, all the time. I've got pictures." I'd specialized in them, after leaving the Pack. The roses that covered my wolf-prints on my chest were so much bigger and darker than they'd had to be—I'd made a point of learning and practicing cover-ups after that, to save others from the mistakes other artists had inflicted on me. I opened my portfolio to show her before and after photos.

"Nice," she said, flipping a page.

"What do you want covered up?"

"This one." She held up her arm, revealing a paw print, exactly same as mine had been.

"Where did you get that?" I asked, trying to keep my voice steady.

"From a friend. It was a bad idea—late at night, lot of drinking, you know how it is."

"Yeah," I said with a quaver. Because she hadn't come in on a motorcycle, Mark's protection had let her walk right on by. "I'm sorry—I'm booked—but Mattie can," I began. Mattie was working behind me, I could hear his running guns.

"You're the one I want. You're the one for me." It was her mouth saying the words, but I knew it might as well have been Gray speaking.

"Get out," I whispered.

Her eyes widened in surprise. "What?"

Was I over-reacting? What if she were just some shittily tattooed stranger? What if—my wolf pushed forward as I took my next inhale. Underneath the cigarettes was a current of animal musk—not dog, not cat—my wolf knew her own.

"Get out," I growled louder, with *her* in my throat.

The skinny girl's eyes narrowed. "Make me."

"Get out!" I shouted at her in a voice not of my own, pointing at the door. The girl jumped back in fear, staring at me, and then ran for it. Seeing all this, my watcher finally got out of his car.

"What happened?" Mattie appeared at my side.

I took control back of my body. "She—she was rude to me." I hugged myself again.

He looked me up and down. "Are you okay?"

"Yeah." Through my new glass windows I could see Mark's man considering going after the girl, who was running down the side-walk. He decided to stay outside, protecting me instead. "It's my shop," I said, laying claim to the place, and quieting any dissent.

"It sure is," Mattie said, placatingly.

I went back into my office, took out my bottle of silver, and shoved it into my pocket.

T<small>HE REST</small> of the day flew by, because of *her* there. Now that I'd let her out inside, I could feel her eyes watching through mine, attracted to the speed of passing cars, her assessing each new client's smell. We had different ideas about what made people attractive—she liked sweat much more than I did—but by the end of the day I felt like I could rely on her. I may not have understood *her* completely, but I felt sure she was trying.

The driver followed me to Rabbit's school then home afterwards and Rabbit, bless his heart, never once looked back, telling me about his day with all the enthusiasm a boy could muster. "And I did what that guy said!"

"What guy?" I asked him, a little too sharply.

His face scrunched in consternation. "The one from last night? Who ate dinner?"

And not some random biker. I downshifted. "His name is Mark—what'd you do, baby?"

"I made friends with some of the other kids Molly picks on. I ate lunch with them, and she pretended not to see me."

"Good job," I said, reaching over to ruffle his hair.

W<small>E ATE</small> dinner alone that evening. I hadn't called Mark all day—I didn't know why, some attempt to seem self-sufficient, I guess—and after eating, once Rabbit had helped with dishes and had bounded back upstairs, my mother asked the question I knew she'd been sitting on since last night.

"So, did he stay over?" she said, giving me a smile halfway between a grin and a leer.

I flushed from my head to my toes. "For a little."

"Good," she said. "And you can tell him I said that."

"Thanks, Mom." I fought not to roll my eyes and went upstairs to hide.

OVER THE COURSE of the next two hours, everyone else in my house was tucked into bed except for me and *her*. I lay down on top of my rumpled sheets, all my clothing still on, and stared at my phone.

Had Mark given up on me? Had I gotten too complicated? Had the Pack gone after him first? I stood up and went to the windows, staring out from in-between the blinds, trying to tell which car in the lot outside was the one with the driver, wondering if it was the same one as before. I watched a car glide in and skip open spots to pause near the curb at the same time as my phone buzzed. I lifted it and saw a text from Mark: *You up?*

I texted him back: *Yes but shhh*, and saw him get out of the car.

I crept downstairs and had the door open by the time he got there. He filled the doorway and then came in, swallowing me in his arms. "The driver told me what happened—are you okay?"

I nodded. "The Pack sent someone over to ask me to do a cover-up. She didn't threaten me or anything. Just trying to scare me more."

"Because *they're* scared, Angie," Mark said.

"Of what?" I asked.

He gave me a smile that said he couldn't tell me. "Stuff and things."

I sighed and nestled my head against his shoulder. His hands rose, one of them moving up to cradle the back of my neck. "I've been thinking about you all day," he whispered in my ear. I knew what he meant by the tone of his voice. My knees went weak, and inside *her* tail swung low.

"Want to tell me about it?"

"I'd rather show you," he said, lifting my chin to kiss my lips. I kissed him back eagerly, pressing my whole body against his. His arms pulled me close, one hand going down to grab my ass and pull my hips towards his. I wound my arms up around his neck, one hand down his back, the other in his hair, pulling my head slightly back then pushing in again, letting my mouth make promises for the rest of my body. He reared his head back, separating us to stare down at me, and made an appreciative sound.

"Shh," I reminded him, as he loosened his tie. He unthreaded it from his collar and held it out like a piece of rope in both hands, then he reached for me, angling it straight like the bit from a bridle. I opened my mouth for it and let him push it in, feeling him tie it firmly behind my hair.

"Good," he said, surveying me afterwards. "Because I'm going to make you want to scream. Get your ass upstairs," he whispered, and I ran to do as I was told.

CHAPTER EIGHT
ANGELA

I reached my bedroom before Mark, of course. I could sense him taking his time, relishing his control over me—just as much as I relished someone else being in control. I didn't know what to do while I waited—but I knew I did want to skip to the screaming part as quickly as possible, so I pulled off all my clothes.

When Mark reached the door of my bedroom he found me sitting on my bed, naked except for the tie that bowed me like a present. At the sight of me waiting, he grinned, and closed the door very quietly behind himself.

"Bounce on that bed for me?" he asked. I did so, feeling my breasts bob—and hearing the springs creak. "That's what I was afraid of," he said, gesturing me toward him with one crooked finger. I stood up and trotted over, doing my best to look both innocent and adorable. It was working, I could hear him breathe harder as he thought of all the different ways he could fuck me.

Which meant that, despite my nudity and my gag, I was still the one in control. I made a show of twisting from side to side, running my hands up and down my body, cradling a breast, pulling a nipple, fingering my clit. He watched in delight, and then

I saw what I wanted—I had a full length mirror that rested on the floor on the far wall of my room. I used it every morning when I got dressed to see all of me—now I wanted to use it to see all of him.

I walked away from him, very deliberately, and got on all fours in front of it, bending my body down and pushing my ass up, begging him to use me.

Mark got the idea at once. He unbuttoned the front of his shirt, so that I could see the rippling muscles leading down to his waist where he unfastened his slacks and unzipped his fly. Normally I'd rush to suck on him, wanting to feel his hot cock fill my mouth, but with the gag on that wasn't an option—so all I did was sway my ass from side to side.

He reached down, not for himself but for me, stroking my pussy, rubbing my clit. Animal instinct came over me and I arced my hips up and leaned back into him, pressing into his hand harder.

"You're so beautiful, Angela," Mark said, looking at the mirror version of me, bowed and bound. I looked over my shoulder at him, urging him with my eyes. He grinned at this, and crawled forward, taking hold of his cock to tease it down my folds.

I went still as nerves lit up in hope, then I rocked back for more. His hands stopped me. "What made you think this was your ride?" he asked, knowing full well I couldn't answer, taking my ass in his hands, tilting it up and spreading it. He started to bob the tip of his cock in and out of me, just the merest fraction of his head, as I moaned.

"Shh, remember?" he reminded me with a tease.

Every time his head dove in my pussy clenched to keep it there, squeezing around him, and he liked that, I knew he did, I heard him moan. Slowly, with more patience than I ever would've had, he crept up behind me, his eyes not on the mirror but on the place where we met, where my pussy grabbed him. When he finally reached his hilt he stopped and leaned forward, undoing the bow of his tie, pulling each end back like they were reins.

He yanked me onto him as he thrust up. I ground helplessly against him, wanting more.

"Do you like that?" he asked, and I nodded imperceptibly against the tie's tension. "Good," he answered, and began to thrust. I could see him in the mirror, the very image of concentration, both of the ends of the tie in one of his hands while his other hand moved my ass to see me. In the mirror I looked beautiful but disheveled, wild as my hair slipped out of place, the tie in my mouth forcing me to pant —and suddenly my wolf was there. Inside me, filling my skin, taking over. We yanked forward, as if to run—and Mark hauled us back, redoubling his efforts, making his cock thump deep inside of me on the spot that wanted me to come.

I could've fought her for control—I'd done it before, banishing her—but she'd protected me today. So as Mark's hands crept up his reins, pulling my head up, fucking me faster, harder—I dropped my reins inside that held her.

All my muscles stiffened and twitched as she came forward, like she was creeping of a dark cave and into the light. I couldn't let go entirely—after so long in control I didn't know how—but I could feel her presence inhabiting me, almost like I was reading her thoughts. For her, every moment of this experience was new—I'd never let her be so free before. Did she want this, like I wanted this? I saw Mark in the mirror through her eyes, the giant alpha of a man who was fucking me. She was so strong, yes, but even the strongest sometimes wanted to be taken.

Mark, as if sensing a change in me, let go of the tie entirely and went for my hair, pulling it back, plunging into me again and again, until instead of rocking apart we were rocking together, he and I, in some primal mating dance and I—*she*—felt things swell and pull and suck and *oh God then we were coming, coming so hard*—if I hadn't had to be quiet I would've shouted, as it was, with her so near inside it was hard not to howl—and wetness spilled down between our thighs, in a hot gush.

"Oh, Angela," Mark purred, pulling himself slowly out. I watched him, mystified to see his cock still hard, as he surveyed me. "I made you squirt." His hand went for the wetness between my thighs and slicked it up again. "That was beautiful," he said, his voice full of reverence.

"Thank you," I whispered back, momentarily overcome. It was like both of us had come inside, like orgasming in stereo. I smiled up at him. "Now...about making you squirt," I teased, as I turned on all fours to address his cock.

I licked it carefully, and felt her inside me, as if *scenting it* and *tasting it* for the first time, before we drew it in, and as we grew bolder, started to suck. I could hear-feel her thoughts—*fangless mouth*—*alpha thrusting*—as Mark made low sounds. If he was happy, we were happy—and what we were doing pleased him.

"I'm loving this view," he said, looking over our ass into the mirror to see our swollen pussy's reflection. He reached forward to grab our haunches again and stretch them wide so he could see everything. A tail we didn't have swung high.

His cock was buried in our mouth and our nose was thick with the *scent of him* when he pulled out abruptly, changing his mind.

"Mmm?" I made the sound into a question as I licked my lips.

"I swear I've never seen you hotter." He reached back to grab pillows off our bed and settle them behind himself as he laid down at an angle, his torso propped up, his cock still hard. "I want to watch you come again—ride me and rub yourself."

I grinned at him, and moved to sit across his hips, our back to him, facing the mirror—and we reached down between our legs to push his cock in.

"Oh yeah," he breathed, as he slid in. *Mounting again—mating again!*—and we relished feeling him anew. We rose up and down on our knees, kneeling above him watching his cock slide in and out in the mirror as we felt it. Watching it somehow made everything feel more real—as though I were me and my reflection was *hers*—and I sank my other hand down to stroke his balls, in a distinctly un-wolf-like move. "Oh—Angela," he breathed, his gaze heavy on us in the mirror, moving from our ass as it faced him, our waist that his hands grabbed, and the image of us rocking on and off of him. I made him watch us lick our fingers and then reach down to rub just like he'd told us, making everything else bright and sharp—the slipperiness of our saliva and our juices letting our fingertips move faster.

"God, baby," he whispered as we felt it building. I could feel my wolf inside, almost growling low—*alpha, alpha, alpha*—almost in a croon, begging him to fuck and claim us, and I took our hand back from his balls to hold a breast and stroke a nipple, as he started thrusting instead of us rocking, his hands holding our waist tight, making us take his cock—we curled forward, legs splayed wide, our knees outside his thighs, as he thrust into us madly, rutting with all his might and—

We gasped, a soundless scream as we came *hard,* catching ourselves before we fell with one hand, still stroking ourselves with the other as his cock rammed us through, so much friction, everything feeling so good—until he grunted, his hands trapping us low as his hips thrust high, his face the picture of determination in reflection, and in the mirror we could see his balls lift and spasm as they filled us with his cum. *Mounted—mated—alpha*—my wolf's thoughts jumbled around in my mind.

I gently fell backwards and sideways, feeling him slide out as we collapsed to the floor, the same time as my wolf receded. I could almost feel her licking her chops as she left, like she'd just eaten a fine meal.

"Christ," Mark muttered, looking at our reflection together in the mirror. He reached down to pull one of my legs up, so that he could see his cum leaking out of me. "Every time I fuck you, Angie—every time."

MARK MADE room on the pillows, but I used his shoulder instead. "How was your day, dear?" I asked, the momentary embodiment of a

1950's housewife—and definitely not a werewolf, in any way, shape, or form. He snorted and turned toward me fully.

"I want to take you out tomorrow night."

"I can't. My mom has her book club."

"Get a babysitter." I gave him a look that let him know how preposterous that sounded. "My driver's going to be here either way," he went on.

"The same driver that let some Pack-related tweaker threaten me?"

"That was a mistake. It won't happen again." He caught my chin and made me look him in the eyes. "I swear I won't let anything happen to you or Rabbit."

Emotions radiated off of him in a wave. He was sincere, yes, but also possessive in a way that I liked, and I knew he meant every word that he'd said.

I gave him a tentative smile. "Good, because now he's building a gang. Of friends, but, a gang nonetheless."

"So come out with me." Mark smiled back, softly. "I want Gray to know you're mine."

I wriggled against him in protest. "You don't know how dangerous that is, Mark."

"In a day or two, it won't be. And the man who threatens my girl —I want him to die without hope."

He said it like a solemn promise, and the word 'die' stilled my squirming. He knew I'd heard it, and I knew I'd heard it and—after today, after Wade's severed organ, after visiting prison and Dark Ink's broken window, and after everything Gray had put unwitting Willa through, and every other moment of my Pack-tinged past—I knew that that death was what it would take, to protect Rabbit and I's future. "Okay," I whispered.

"Okay?" he asked, giving me my last out.

"Yeah," I said, tucking my chin down against him. He kissed my forehead and pulled me tight.

CHAPTER NINE
JACK

I checked my phone in Vermillion's parking lot. Three missed calls from Paco, no texts, no voicemail messages—*shit*.

"Hey," I said, calling him immediately back. "You all right?"

"Yeah. I just kind of wanted to tell you this in person."

I sagged with relief. "What?"

"I'm ninety-five percent sure my current boss is banging your boss, at this very moment."

I leaned on the door of my vintage black Lincoln Continental. "Remind me again who that is?"

"Mark Carrera. Big guy. Lawyer?"

"Ah." I got inside my car and turned the engine on. "They've been dating for a few months, Paco—this isn't exactly new news." I knew if I were dating Angela, I'd be taking her body out for a test drive three times a night.

"No, but the fact that I'm supposed to be watching her overnight afterwards is. I'm not his driver tonight, Jack—I'm muscle."

I turned the engine off so I could hear him better. "Why? What's he expecting to go down?"

"Don't know. His driver will be back for him, but I'm supposed to sit out here all night, waiting."

"Armed?"

"Of course."

"I'm on my way over," I said, and hung up before he could tell me otherwise.

I KNEW WHERE ANGELA LIVED, and once I got there it wasn't hard to find Paco's dark car. I parked three rows away, heard his doors unlock as I walked over, and sidled into the passenger seat after giving the lot a look-around.

One of Paco's guns was in his lap, and another one was holstered at his side. "You weren't kidding," I said.

"Nope." Paco looked at me, expression serious. "Does this have anything to do with the information you requested from me?"

"About the Pack? Why would it?"

"Because my mission tonight is to keep her safe from Pack members. Bikers, gangsters, and guys—or girls—who look like they used to be in prison."

"Christ." I sank into the seat. Was it coincidence? Or did Angela and Bella have something in common? I turned toward him. "If you see a Pack member, you have to stay away from him, Paco."

Paco gave me a *look*. "I can handle a leather suited alcoholic."

"Not one who changes into a wolf on a full moon night," I said, my voice grave.

His eyes narrowed. "You're kidding me," he said, but I knew he'd believe.

"I wish I were. I underestimated one recently—I don't think he could've killed me, but he could've killed you, twice."

Paco grimaced, then shrugged. "I've got silver shot back home." My eyes widened as he went on. "What? I know you have enemies,

Jack. I want to help you fight them. You can't blame me for being prepared."

I clapped a hand over his mouth. "Don't tell me anything else. Anything you tell me, she can make me tell her." It was clear over the course of our relationship I'd already told him far too much. He nodded slowly and I took back my hand. "You can't interrupt my job tonight, Jack. I have a professional rep to uphold."

"I won't," I lied, prepared to sit here and protect him and Angela until dawn. Then another car swooped in.

"Driver," Paco said. "Get down."

I ducked low so that Mark's other employee wouldn't see me and I pulled out my phone. If Mark was on his way out...I stayed low until I heard a car door swing open and then shut. I started texting Angela right afterwards: *Don't suppose you're still up?*

By the time I was straight in the seat again I had my reply.

Yeah. You?

Always. Can we talk? In person? I'm close.
A longer pause.

Sure. Don't ring—just text once you're outside.

"That is such a bad idea, Jack," Paco said, reading over my shoulder.

"You're just jealous," I said, leaning over to kiss him before getting out of the car.

I WAITED a likely amount of time before taking the cement stairs up two at a time and standing outside her door.

Here, I texted.

The door slowly opened and Angela stepped outside, closing it softly behind her. She was barefoot and wearing a loosely cinched white robe, her hair tousled in thick waves. There was something wild and beautiful about her, and even though she stank of another man, I wanted her. At seeing me in person, she looked a little panicked.

"I was driving nearby," I explained, trying to allay her fears. "And I was wondering—"

"When you could go back to work," she finished for me, and frowned. "Sorry, I've just been so busy with personal things."

"Like what?" I asked, imploring her to tell me with my eyes. As if she sensed that, she sank back.

"It's just been weird—and busy."

"Did you figure out who broke the window?"

"No, not yet."

She was lying, I knew it. I wished I could tell her that, somehow make her give the truth to me. My truth was I didn't want to go back to work until things were solved, the twin mysteries of her and Bella's problems with the pack. But if I didn't pretend to want to work, I had no excuse to be here. "How much longer do you think things'll be?"

"Another day or two."

"What's going to change by then?" The look on her face said she couldn't tell me. "Angela, what the hell's going on?" I asked, stepping forward.

Her back pressed against the door behind her, as her hand found the knob. "I can't tell you, so don't ask. I just don't want anyone to be in danger," she said, then quickly followed it up with, "I mean working at night there—there's a reason I don't give Charla the night shifts and—"

Which was bullshit, meant to cover things up. I was so tempted to whammy her, but her next question distracted me. "What're you doing tomorrow night?" she asked.

"Nothing," I answered quickly, hoping she wanted me to do something with her.

"Can you do me a big favor then? I need someone to watch Rabbit for me—my mom's going out."

"Yeah," I said, reflexively. Anything to get in her good graces. I chuckled. "And you think I'm not in danger with him? You've obviously never tried to play video games with him before."

She put a hand to her mouth to stifle a laugh and gave me a complicated look. "Just give me a little longer Jack. Don't give up on me, okay?"

"I won't," I said—and meant it. Then the moment between us stretched a little too long.

"So, I," she said, her hand twisting her door knob and ducking her head down.

"Yeah." I flipped out my phone and checked the time of tomorrow's sunset minus a shower. "I can't be here until six-forty-five."

"Seven's fine."

"Okay. Seven it is."

"Thanks Jack." She opened up the door behind her and stepped halfway inside.

"You're welcome," I whispered, and waited until she was safe inside and I heard her lock the door.

I STOPPED by Paco's car on my way to my own—he rolled down the passenger window and let me lean in. "Well?" he asked.

"I'm watching Rabbit—her kid—tomorrow night."

Paco was aghast. "You are a dumb motherfucker."

"Not with her yet."

He rolled his eyes. "What does a vampire know about babysitting a child? Stick your head in here farther so I can roll the window up and decapitate you."

"I've hung out with him before at the shop. It'll be easy, and then I can be there, just in case."

"When's the last time you fed?"

I knew he wasn't offering. "I can manage for a night." He stared me down. "It'll be fine," I protested.

"Well if it's not, you've got my number. Call me."

"I wasn't aware that babysitting was in your repertoire." I cocked an eyebrow.

He made a face. "At least I have base mammalian instincts."

I pulled back, wounded. "That's low."

"It was," he apologized, after a deep inhale. "I'm sorry."

I didn't think it was just the shock of my actions making him snappish—I think while I'd been talking to Angela, Paco'd been thinking about being out here without silver shot. "I'll call you and let you know how things go."

"Good."

I rocked back and tapped the side of his car like a highway patrolman. "I think we're done here. Get back to work."

He flashed me a dark look and then pressed the button to roll the window up.

CHAPTER TEN
ANGELA

I leaned against the far side of the door the second Jack left, my heart still in my throat. My wolf—it'd been so strange—at first seeing Jack, my wolf had lunged like a dog on a leash, angry and afraid. Of Jack, of all people, one of my oldest employees, someone I knew—and that she ought to recognize! It'd been hard to carry on a rational conversation with him over *her* fear—especially as it twisted and changed through ten different other emotions, calming down to wind up at...lust. By the end of our conversation, she'd *wanted* him.

I frowned at myself, as I pushed off the door and went to take the stairs. Maybe she wasn't picky now that I'd finally let her out, and she wanted to catch up on all the life she'd missed while I'd trapped her with silver deep inside.

Or—I walked into my room, past the painting of a rabbit Jack had meticulously done as a gift for me—maybe my wolf sensed something in him, like I thought I did sometimes. Something bad... but also good.

I went to the window to peek through the blinds. Jack was out in the parking lot talking to the guys Mark had left behind. I wondered if he was getting interrogated on my behalf—one of my own employees! How was I going to explain that to Jack if he asked later? I couldn't breathe a word of what Mark was doing for me, I'd have to come up with a decent lie by the time I saw Jack again tomorrow night.

The smell of sex here was still heady in the air—I crawled back into bed with my robe still on, one knee bent. Jack's arrival had brought *her* back in full-force and now she was still roiling around inside, reveling in her freedom within me—and thinking about Jack.

"Don't be silly," I told her, pulling one hand up to my robe's v-neck. The skin there—my skin—was so soft. I wondered if I'd ever appreciated that before—and then realized that that was her thought, that just as I marveled in her fur, she could be mystified at my smoother parts. My hand stroked out and down a little as if of its own accord, tracing up the slight peak to my still hidden nipple.

I opened up my mouth to chastise her—and then realized I'd never given her a name. Did she have one? Would I find out if I asked her? One fingertip played lazily against the cotton, relishing the sensations underneath.

"Girl," I warned, and got a flood of impressions from her. What if Jack were in the room, what if Jack was beside us, what if it were him here, doing this, to us? Whatever affection she'd shown Mark was utterly redoubled where Jack was concerned. I sidled off the shoulder of my robe without thinking about it, giving my hands more range.

"That's impossible," I told her. "And it's silly."

But I didn't stop as we traced the outline of a breast. We wriggled, and the entire top of our robe came off, both arms free now, hands able to stroke and pull and touch. Sensations rolled over my body, electric because I was feeling them twice, once through me and once through her.

I closed my eyes as my hands crept south and imagined him behind me, that I could feel him breathing as he explored me, and my other knee came up. I pushed the robe's soft cotton away and down, so that the only bit of it still on me was the tie across my waist, and I imagined that that pressure somehow were his arms as one of my fingers reached my clit.

After everything that'd come before this evening I should've had nothing left, and yet—touching there, stroking gently on top of my hood   everything in me came back to life. Oh, if only it were Jack's tongue—I gave into my wolf's imagination, letting her images roll through me—realizing that most of them were thoughts I'd already had before. Him below me on the bed, kissing up, pushing his tongue in *there*—as I pushed eager fingers inside. The way I knew he'd kiss my clit, rolling it against his tongue—as I used my own juices to smoothly slick it in his stead. My left hand crossed my chest to grab at my right breast, stroking, rubbing, and pulling, as the other one danced in the rhythm of my imagination, using three fingers to rub myself luxuriantly in slow wide circles.

If it were his hands on me—I'd seen them often enough with their tattoos—if it was his body below me, so that I could look down at the markings on his chest—if it was his body above me, his cock thrusting in—I pushed my fingers lower to mimic the effect, feeling how wet I was, how ready, if only instead of sending him away I'd pulled him in.

But no—I belonged to Mark—even as I imagined Jack breathlessly kissing me, grabbing my hips, pulling me onto him as I rose up on my toes, our bodies joined. I kept my eyes screwed shut, picturing him taking me, the way his eyes would be looking down, so pleased to be inside me at long last—

And that was it, wasn't it. He'd smelled of other women tonight —so many other women! All the time! But he still wanted *me*. He'd never said anything about it after he'd started working for me, but I could see it in his eyes. I could feel him watching me when we were both at the shop, when he thought I didn't know. On the surface we kept it professional, but underneath—he was a man who desperately wanted to fuck me, and I was a werewolf who desperately wanted to be fucked. Tonight had been no different.

My hands took on a life of their own, playing me, pulling me closer to the edge as I gave in—Jack's lips at my neck, my hands in his hair, him hard inside—I went deeper, pressed harder and thought of him coming inside me with a wild cry, so eager to give me his load—it was that that made me come, my hips shaking as my breath hissed, the thought of me taking it inside, that final moment when his cock would be ramrod straight before coming in me.

My hands carried me through, and I pressed my knees together for a moment, sealing my fingers in and rocking myself. Pleasure and relief rolled through me in equal waves, until I collapsed. Instead of getting up to turn the light off, I put a pillow over my head and went to sleep, deeply satisfied.

CHAPTER ELEVEN
JACK

I pulled my car into the parking lot at my own apartment complex wondering if Paco was right. I only had a few hours left till dawn if I was going to shirk kid-duty. I didn't want to be an asshole and cancel late—but how hard could watching one seven-year-old be? I put my car into park and got out.

A red Honda civic turned to pull in and park right beside mine, the only other vacant spot. I got out of the way and gave a neighborly nod—to Florida.

"Hey," he said, getting out of his car quickly.

"Hey," I said back. He was wearing an outfit, the livery of some hotel downtown, and he noticed me noticing.

"I'm on lunch break."

"So you are," I said, gave him a companionable grin, and started heading for my number.

"It's thirty minutes," he said, almost to the back of my head. I could've kept walking but—Paco had a point. If I wasn't going to get the chance to feed tomorrow night, I needed to die at dawn full.

And also he looked fucking good in black.

I turned very slowly, walked back to the space between our cars, and got far too close to him. "How hungry are you?" I asked, my voice low.

His lips parted in anticipation. "I don't need to eat any food," he said, and reached for my belt. He had it unbuckled and was about to kneel down when I remembered where I'd been earlier.

"Come here," I said, pulling him up and closer to me, undoing his own belt and pants. He made a small noise as my hand sank in, and as I found the heat of his cock I felt it swell. "I don't have much time, again," I said, whispering, pressing his head to mine, nuzzling his ear. "So this is going to be fast, yeah? Lips later, sucking later—fast for now."

He nodded—and then his own hand pushed into my jeans to grasp me. I was instantly hard and heard him moan, thinking of so many other things we could do. "Not today," I whispered, and pulled his hand out as I began to stroke him.

Florida was easy to read—between his posture and his breath, the way his blood flew around inside him like he was a snowglobe, the thickness of his cock against my palm—he was mine to control, and I could make this experience last as long as it pleased me or make him instantly come. I played with him, bringing him close, listening to his breath catch and him almost whine, taking him further and further repeatedly—it was like his orgasm was a ripening plum—I wanted to push it to the limit until it was the right time to taste.

"Please, please, please," his hips beat against my hand, begging as he did for release.

"Okay," I breathed, and gave him it, two more firm strokes from hilt to head and—he gasped and sagged against me, curling up, making all sorts of soft noises.

"Shh," I counseled, feeling his cock go rigid and then hot cum spill into my hand in pulses. Life reverberated out of him like a firmly plucked bass string, deep and true. I basked in it as I pulled him forward, so his cum would fall between us, missing his crisply ironed slacks. Then I gently let go of him and flicked my hand to knock the rest of it to the ground. He stood there, balanced against his car, hands on his thighs, panting. "What's your name?"

"Zach."

"We're not going to make this a thing okay, Zach? I have friends and obligations." I wiped my hand on my jeans as he caught his breath. He nodded.

"I just feel bad," he said, and made a gesture towards me, where I was redoing my belt, clearly hard myself.

"Don't," I said too firmly, and he looked hurt. "Maybe I like having you owe me," I added, to soften it.

He almost laughed then. "If you say so."

"I do. Have a good night, Zach," I said, going for my keys with my clean hand.

"What's your name?"

"Maybe I'll tell you next time," I said, without looking back.

I took the long way to get to my apartment, not that he was in any shape to follow me, and locked myself inside with an irate Sugar.

"I know, I know, I was gone all night, I'm sorry, okay?" I apologized as she wound against my calves, meowing. I washed my hands and was booting up my computer to kill time till dawn when on my desk my phone buzzed. A text, from Paco—hopefully apologizing for being a jerk.

I opened it up and read:

Hey, new intel from coroner's office.

I was typing out *Yeah?* when his next text arrived.

Bella was knocked up.

I replaced my *Yeah?* with a *Thanks.*

Bella was pregnant? How far along was she when I was with her? I tried to think back. She'd always had a few curves, but nothing I would've asked about—and it would have been none of my business besides. But if she'd really known what the Pack was, and had somehow been impregnated with a werewolf child, that might explain why she'd gone on the run—and why Pack members would want to chase her.

I tried to braid the threads together in my mind, Bella's death, Angela hiding out from the Pack—was she pregnant with a werewolf's baby too? No. She'd been with Mark for months, and while he had a jaw like a lantern, I felt confident that if I punched it hard enough it'd shatter.

But she did already have a child—Rabbit. And she had gotten that strange letter from prison....

I had a wild hunch—and suddenly it was a good thing I was watching Rabbit tomorrow night—all the better to try and touch him with something silver.

CHAPTER TWELVE
JACK

I woke up in my coffin substantially less convinced that trying to burn my boss's theoretically werewolf son with silver was a good idea. Sugar heard me breathing and started meowing for food.

"All right, all right." I pushed my way out of the box that I'd died in at dawn and made my way to the kitchen to feed her.

Sugar wasn't the only one who was hungry. I didn't have to eat tonight, I'd kept my hunger topped off recently with sex, but Paco was right—I was stronger when I'd freshly bled someone. I just hadn't bothered cultivating too many of those connections when sex was so easy to find. It still would be, except for the fact that I needed to go watch a seven year old in forty-five minutes. Maybe I should've gotten Zach's apartment number....

I walked out of the kitchen and toward the shower, past my front door—which had a note slid underneath it.

Check under your hood - P

I bit my lip, wondering what Paco had put there for me, and hopped into the shower.

Twenty minutes later I was outside with wet hair and my hood popped up looking at a folded towel. I took it, closed the hood, and sat inside my car before opening it—revealing a six inch knife in a boot holster. It sizzled when I touched it—silver for sure—and I smiled. I'd take weaponry over an apology any day.

ANGELA

"ANGELA, what does Jack possibly know about watching a child?" Mark asked, his expression halfway between a laugh and a frown.

Good question. Asking Jack to watch Rabbit while Mark and I went out wasn't a decision I could entirely defend. "Look, this was last minute, and he was available. Plus, I felt bad for him, he hasn't worked since the windows were broken."

"So you're paying him?"

"No." I hadn't even thought about that angle. "Should I?"

Mark decided to laugh. "Well if your son's anything like you, he can watch himself. Plus I'll leave a driver outside," he said, with intent. I had no doubt that in addition to knowing CPR, the driver was probably armed. "I'm not going to let anything stand in the way of me taking you out tonight."

And I knew why. I licked my lips. Something was going to go down with Gray in prison in the next few days, courtesy of Mark's connections, and then I'd finally be free. I wouldn't have to live the rest of my life wondering when Gray was going to get out or who he was going to send after me. Rabbit and I would never have to worry again. I didn't know how badly I'd wanted that until now, when it was almost in my grasp.

Mark watched me thinking and tilted his head down. "You okay?"

"Yeah. I am—I really am," I said, giving him a shy smile, right as the doorbell rang.

Rabbit thundered down the stairs, excited to have company. "Can I get it?"

I blocked his path instinctively. "No." *Not yet. But soon*, I wanted to tell him. I turned around and opened the door up myself.

Jack stood outside looking out of place and smelling like soap. "Hey," he said, with a low wave, acknowledging all three of us.

"Hey," I said back, pulling into my apartment to let him in.

"Jack!" Rabbit shouted in delight.

"Hey Rabbit," Jack said back, smiling at him.

A slight flush rose as I remembered my imagination the prior night, but luckily the men were too busy sizing one another up to notice. It was so strange that my wolf thought Jack and Mark were equals, when Mark had four inches and a hundred extra pounds on Jack, easy.

"You're really going to babysit me tonight?" Rabbit asked, looking back and forth between us, unable to believe his good luck.

"Yep! And he's going to have you in bed by nine," I said, giving Jack a look.

"Hi Mark," Jack said, putting his hand out.

"Jack," Mark said, shaking it.

"How late are y'all gonna stay out?" Jack asked, companionably, with a hint of his southern twang.

"My mother will be back around ten—you can take off then," I said, ducking down to tug the strappy backs of my heels up.

"It's okay if she's later than that," Jack said with a shrug.

I grinned. "She's pushing seventy. She doesn't stay out late, unlike some people."

Mark made a face like he was going to say something particularly manly, and I started pushing on his chest with both hands. "Bye! Stay out of trouble!" I said, and shoved us out the door. When it snicked behind me and I heard it lock, I started to relax. Mark, however, kept looking back behind us on the way to the parking lot.

"What do you really know about him, anyhow?" he asked.

My wolf says he's safe. "I know all I need to," I said, giving him a mysterious grin, before ducking into his car.

CHAPTER THIRTEEN
JACK

I'd only gotten glimpses of the inside of Angela's apartment before, and here I was, finally in the inner sanctum. Rabbit ran off upstairs. "So where's your grandma tonight?" I shouted after him.

"Book club."

"Is she really gonna be out till ten?"

"Prolly!" Rabbit shouted back, before reappearing and thundering down. "Can I show you some stuff?"

He wanted to be liked so badly that he was impossible not to like. Rabbit had fine blonde hair, pale skin like his mother's, and eyes as gray as a thunderstorm. I grinned at him. "Only if afterwards I can show *you* some things."

"Okay!" he said, grabbed my hand, and started hauling me upstairs.

Rabbit's room was any seven year old's dream—his mother had painted the walls to look like outer space, black with bright supernovas, swirls of distant galaxies, the deep red of a bursting sun, and his sheets were rocket-ship patterned. All things my parents would've never bothered to do.

Being seven, he took all this for granted.

"Wow—Rabbit," I said with a low whistle, spinning to take it all in.

"What?"

"That's pretty cool," I said, gesturing at the walls.

He glanced up from the toy pile where he was digging for something special to display. "I guess." He pulled out a dinosaur with a jetpack. "But this is cooler!"

I sat down on his bed. "You're right," I agreed.

For half an hour we looked at different toys and made them attack each other. I followed along with his imagination, trying to keep up as we went from trying to survive an alien invasion to biting someone named Molly, to racing because we were being chased by a dog the size of a house and had been thrown into the past. At the end of it I fell onto his twin bed in defeat, pretending to die in dramatic fashion, which was ironic since up until about ninety minutes ago I actually had been dead—and from my vantage point I noticed a break in the black wall, presumably the door to a bathroom.

"Okay. The aliens have won," I said, sitting up.

"They can't win, Jack. You have to keep fighting!"

"I'm dead," I groaned.

"No you're not! It was just poison! You had an antidote!"

"I did?"

"Yep!"

I shook my head and rocked to standing. "Well, all right then— but recently dead people sometimes need to pee."

"The bathroom's over there," he said, and started industriously lining up more toys.

I casually leaned forward like I was taking off a boot, but instead of doing that brought out the knife Paco had given me, and tossed it out onto the bed behind me in an easy arc. Then I slowly walked to the bathroom, closed the door behind myself, and listened against it with an ear.

Any minute now.

I was a little disgusted with myself, waiting for a friend's child to accidentally touch something possibly painful but—how else was I to know? If I whipped it out and given it to him to touch, he'd tell his mom for sure—I had to have some plausible deniability—although if he ever told Angela, it was likely I'd never get back inside Dark Ink, much less her apartment. After three minutes of mostly silence I leaned over, flushed the toilet, and walked back out, prepared to take it away from him safely, expecting to find him using it to pry the saddle off a dino-charger.

Instead, I walked back into the room and saw it sitting where I'd tossed it on his bed. "Didn't you see that?" I asked, pointing at it.

"Yeah."

"Do you know what it is?"

"Yeah."

"Well...why aren't you playing with it?"

He was stacking dinosaurs up on top of one another to make a mega-dino and didn't even turn toward me to talk. "My mom told me not to play with knives."

And there was the difference between Rabbit's upbringing and mine, in a nutshell. If I'd been given a knife, I probably would've hid it in my mattress and dreamed about using it on my frequently angry father. What the hell had I been thinking anyways? I swooped it up and clipped it back in my boot.

"I'm hungry," Rabbit announced, looking to me for food.

Me too, kid. But I knew somewhere perfect for children to go. "Go get your shoes and a jacket—we're going out."

I wrote Angela's mom a note, tenting it to be easily visible on the counter just in case she got home before us, while Rabbit was running around the house putting clothes on. When I was done with that, I felt my phone buzz—Paco, worried about my non-mammilian instincts.

I'm working my night off tonight, because of you.

I'm flattered.

You'd better be. Everything all right in there?

Peachy. We're heading out.

Why?

Kid's hungry, and I don't remember how to cook.

There are these things called 'microwaves.'

We'll be back by ten, that's when Grandma's getting back.

You think I'm letting you out of my sight?

Don't think you're going to have much choice. We're going to Happyland.

Happyland was one of those places you couldn't get into without a child in tow, all the better to cut down on predators. I'd never been, but the commercials made it look nice.

Thanks for the knife, I texted him, and repocketed my phone.

AFTER A BRIEF TUSSLE which I let him win, I let Rabbit lock his door officially and then stick the key into one of his jacket's many pockets, and together we walked out to my ride.

"Wow—this is yours?" he said, his gray eyes wide.

"All mine," I said, as he ran around outside my 1963 Lincoln Continental, putting handprints on all the smooth black. I'd won it years ago in a private card game—the only time I'd ever used my whammy to cheat. The guy who owned her didn't deserve her, and Betty was worth cheating for.

It was clear from Rabbit's excitement that he'd never been in a real car before—and quite possibly my car had never had a child his age in it. I thought for a dark moment about putting a trashbag underneath him, lest he foul the passenger seat with some child-related effluvia, but decided against it, and let him roll the radio dial from side to side instead, as we shouted over the engine noise.

"This is awesome," he said, when we were three blocks away from his apartment. "My mom never lets me sit in the front seat!"

"Why not?"

"I dunno!"

Because—I realized slowly—letting children his age sit in the front seat was probably illegal. And since my car was from 1963, Betty also didn't have airbags. Not a big deal for me, since I couldn't die, but I realized this was perhaps a worse betrayal of Angela's confidence than leaving Rabbit with a knife. "Hey, Rabbit? Promise me you'll never tell your mom I let you do this."

He started cranking the windows down excitedly—likely he'd never seen a hand-crank either. "Okay!"

HAPPYLAND WAS one of those uniquely Vegas institutions—a children's arcade with an exceptionally strong bar. If you weren't going to get to gamble or see any adult entertainment, at least you wouldn't have to spend your evening sober. I parked and watched Paco's car slide past us in the parking lot.

Rabbit hopped out of the front seat and slammed the door behind him like a king. "Happyland! My mom never takes me here! Not even when the other kids have birthday parties!"

"Well, as you might have noticed, I'm not your mom," I said, grinning at him, as he hovered around me like an errant comet, zooming forward and back as we made our way inside.

"I'm not hungry anymore," Rabbit told me, the second we could hear the bleeps and bloops of the games inside, like Paradise Island siren songs.

"Yeah, I'm not falling for that," I said. I put a hand on his shoulder and steered him into the dining half of the establishment. The entire menu was a kid's menu, with a small 'adult' section, so the roles were reversed. Rabbit contemplated his side of it after we sat down, and I wondered how much he could actually read. "What're you getting?"

"Chicken fingers with ranch."

When the waitress came by, I let him order. "Make it two," I said, giving the woman both our menus. "And please bring extra crayons."

She gave me a flirtatious wink. "You got it."

She returned with crayons, a decaf soda for Rabbit, and a Jack and Coke for me. I could eat and drink, it just didn't do much of anything—and it definitely didn't make me less hungry. Some unconscious part of me kept track of the way the kid in the booth across from us kicked his legs, even as I tried to deny it.

"What're you drawing?" Rabbit asked, looking up from his own placemat, where he, too, had been hard at work.

I hadn't been paying attention much, to be honest. I'd started off with a curve, then another, then bubbled out from there, and was now in the middle of a complicated cloud system which I was shading in—it was about to rain.

"Thunderstorm. You?"

"Your car," he said, holding his placemat up. We hadn't been given black crayons, so he was making do with dark purple.

I grinned at him. "Hey, that's pretty nice—maybe I can keep it."

"Yeah?"

"Yeah. But only if you sign it once you finish. I want a Rabbit original."

He was excited, then turned sly. "You know my mom gets paid for her art...."

"I've got five bucks in my pocket for tokens. That's all you're getting from me."

He laughed, and went back to coloring.

CHAPTER FOURTEEN
ANGELA

Mark was distracted the entire drive to the Strip. "You're more worried about it than I am," I said, trying to tease him. Once again, we pulled into the circle of the Fleur de Lis Hotel. I tried to play it casual and not gawk, but it was hard. "You know you're going to spoil me if you keep taking me here."

He flashed me a grin. "That's kind of what I'm hoping for." And then he went back to distant concentration.

"It's not just Jack, is it," I asked slowly.

"A man of my stature has a lot on his mind," he said, his tone lightly sarcastic.

Like murdering my shitty ex in prison? "I wish I weren't giving you other things to worry about."

His hand reached out for mine. "It's not you—it's never you," he said. He squeezed it, and I squeezed back. We both got out of the car, held hands again, and it was like we'd never let them go at all.

He led us to a back elevator, one you needed a special pass for, and let us take it up. It had a glass front, so we could see the glory of Fleur's casino floor in front of us, and I pressed up against him, momentarily afraid of heights. His arm circled me, hand on my hip, and part of me wanted to squirm and twist to make it cup my ass—my wolf, there again in full force. Where had she been hiding all day? Lying in wait to make her presence known at night? The moon was waxing—maybe it made her more strong.

Mark, knowing none of this, looked over and down as the elevator slowed. He bowed his head to nuzzle his chin against my temple as the elevator doors opened. We were in the VIP entrance of a club and there were only two couples ahead of us, even though the dance floor past them was nearly full.

"Dancing?" I asked, looking up. "You dance?"

"Not well—but I can tell you do. And I want to watch."

"I haven't been dancing in years, Mark," I protested.

"What better night to start up again then?" he said, taking my hand and pulling us to the hostess.

His name was on a list of course, and a girl wearing a very revealing outfit took us to a booth behind the dancefloor, reserved with a velvet rope. She undid this and let us through, where we sat down into plush leather couches in front of a table full of expensive drinks, and Mark set about pouring two for us. He handed me mine as he picked up his and made our glasses clink.

"What are we toasting to this time?"

"Beautiful women and freedom."

I beamed, watching him take a sip. How had I gotten so marvelously lucky—I took a sip of *my* drink and almost sneezed. My wolf was unaccustomed to the bitterness of alcohol. Mark laughed melodiously. "What, you don't believe me?" he teased. "You're the most beautiful woman in this club. Any man here would kill to spend one night with you."

And at that, I laughed. "Mark, don't be silly."

"I'm not," he growled, sounding sure, with a smug grin.

I relaxed back into the couch, crossing my legs so that my skirt hiked up, content to play his game. "Well, of course I could get a guy here, if I wanted. I don't know if you've noticed, but guys don't exactly play hard to get."

He mulled this, swirling his drink. "What would be a better test then? A woman?"

I tensed. I hadn't been with a woman since Willa—and I hadn't told Mark about her, it would've been too complicated. I had a willow tree tattooed on my hip in her honor though—long branches from it swept down my upper thigh—I could see a centimeter of them peeking out from beneath my skirt right now. I reached down to trace their edge without thinking.

What if being with him meant I got to reclaim that part of my life too?

"I didn't mean to push things," Mark said, taking my reflection for refusal.

"No, it's okay." I took a much more measured sip of my drink, warning my wolf to brace. "What would we do with an extra girl?"

His eyebrows rose, not sure if I was tempting or teasing. "Whatever you wanted to do with one?" he guessed, so as not to get into trouble.

"You've done things like that before?"

He nodded subtly. "You?"

I nodded, just as smooth. "It's been a long time though. I could be rusty."

His eyes studied mine, trying to lawyer-judge my intent. "I don't want to push things Angela—I don't want to mess anything up."

Without thinking, I swirled my hand and made the ice in my drink spin. "What if it were me, doing the pushing?"

"If that were true, I wouldn't mind," he said slowly.

"Here's the thing though," I said, setting the glass down. "If I caught one, she'd be mine, for tonight. You wouldn't get to touch her. You might not even get to watch, depending. If I did something like that—I'd just need to see what it was like again."

I could almost watch him doing calculations. "Two caveats then. You don't get her number—and you forget her name."

He was worried he was going to lose me? After everything we'd been through, and everything he'd done—*and was doing!*—for me?

He truly had no idea how loyal I could be. I stood and walked over to him, as his eyes roved up and down me. Could he tell the way my wolf waited just underneath my skin? He was hip height to us now, sitting down, and we looked down at him both teasing and triumphant, and stroked a hand down his cheek. "See you soon, darling."

WITH MY WOLF on board I viewed the entire room through different eyes. She was unsure about what I was asking of us—but she was more than willing to participate if it led to more sex. The urges she had to chase and catch and fuck—they were intense, sometimes so strong I had to stand still and wait for them to pass.

I pushed my way through the crowd of dancers until I reached the bar and ordered another drink, charging it to Mark's table. I saw him across the room, watching me, and saluted him with my glass before looking around.

There were bachelorette parties, even here—and throngs of men with more money than sense, trying to hit on them. For once, I felt some sympathy. Willa and I had practically fallen together—I'd talked a good game in front of Mark, but hitting on strangers wasn't really my thing.

Then again, I didn't know another person here. Even humiliation wouldn't be all that embarrassing—I'd still be going home with Mark. What did I have to lose? Just my pride.

I looked around for someone looking like myself, a little alone, a little lost, and then I saw her. She was a little taller than Willa had been, and slightly heavier. Her wavy blonde hair was asymmetrically cut and shaved up in back, in the way that I knew made me and other people want to touch. She had big earrings and perfectly done up lips. A guy was talking to her and she was sending out every signal in the book that said she wanted nothing to do with him but he was too drunk or too oblivious to notice. The third time she took a step back, hunched over and gave him a 'for the love of God, leave me alone' grimace, I stepped in.

"Hey Christa!" I got in close, like we were friends already. "I've been looking for you! Mel is totally puking in the bathroom, and we've got to go." I dared to put my hand on her arm and feel the softness of her skin.

She knew what I was doing instantly and turned toward me, lighting up. "Oh my God, Samantha, why didn't you find me sooner?"

Her hand slid down my arm and grabbed my hand and pulled us both aside. The oaf tried to follow, but I gave him a stern look. "No. Just *no*," I said—no wolf involved, just angry female—and set him off his game. He was pissed, but by then she was pulling me away and it was too late.

"Oh my gosh, thank you. He's attending the same convention as I am, I couldn't be rude, but ugh." She shuddered lightly, like a horse.

I laughed. "I thought you were putting up the Bat Signal, but if I was wrong, I was prepared to pretend I'd thought you were someone else."

She laughed. "I'm," she began, putting out her hand.

I raised mine instead to cut her off. "How about I just call you Christa tonight?"

One of her eyebrows quirked up. "Do I look like an ex of yours?"

I flushed a little red, but still managed to be bold. "I, uh, made a complicated promise to a friend. I happen to have an extensive credit line here though so if you like high end vodka I could tell you all about it?"

She pushed a wave of her hair behind her ears, measuring me with her eyes. They were wide and cat-like, full of curiosity. "Sure— why not?"

"T<small>HAT IS</small> the most Eyes Wide Shut thing I've ever heard," she said, after I explained my situation with Mark and she was holding a new glass.

"I agree. But I notice you're not running."

"Not yet at least. This," she said, picking up her glass and tilting it toward me, "is excellent. I'm just hoping it's not roophied."

"Oh God no—that would be awful, and cheating."

"And cheating," she mimicked me with a snort, and looked over my shoulder. "So who's the lucky man?"

"He's alone in a booth behind me, wearing a dark blue suit jacket. Probably looking our way."

I saw her eyes flicker and land. "Christ," she muttered.

"Yeah."

"I'm mean, I'm a gold star lesbian, and even I can see the appeal of that."

I chuckled. "There are grades? Why did no one tell me?"

"I'm guessing you weren't a lesbian for very long."

"Bi, more, really."

"Uh huh," she said, curt. "So—you saved me from one man, only to toss me in the lap of another? That's not very nice." Straight, the words would've been rough, but her tone was teasing—and her eyes were flirting with me over the edge of her glass.

"He's not allowed to touch you. Just me."

"And why is that?"

I stared past her for a moment, remembering. "Honestly? Because he sort of dared me to find a woman tonight, and I want to tease him mercilessly. But also—a long time ago a man took someone from me. I don't want to get into it, because it's almost resolved now but...I kind of want to take that part of my life back."

"Someone steal your girl?" she practically purred the words.

Everything I'd ever done with Willa came back, and the memories made me breathless. "Something like that."

Her head tilted to one side, making the drama of her haircut more distinct. "What if you're no good at being with women anymore?"

"Then you tell me so and go."

"What if we have fantastically amazing sex and you realize men are useless?" She gave me a ruthless grin.

"No name, no numbers, no attachments. And—I do love him."

"Strange way of showing it...Samantha."

"We're complicated people, what can I say?" I said, giving her a smile somewhere between hopeful and helpless.

"So it seems," she agreed.

And now, it was time to wait. There wasn't anything else I could explain or say, nothing more she needed to hear. She was either intrigued or she wasn't.

"I'm not used to being other people's play thing," she said, and I started to nod like that was a totally reasonable out. "But...it is Vegas. And it's only one night. And I like the idea of making your man pay."

"For what?"

"For anything. I'm sure he's done some bad stuff," she said, and gave me a wink. "I'm in room two-thirty-eight. How about you and your fellow give me a ten minute head start?" she suggested, and then walked away.

My heart leapt into my throat and started pounding as I watched her go.

CHAPTER FIFTEEN
JACK

R abbit and I ate quickly while he told me about the games he was looking forward to playing—other children had thoroughly explained the magic of Happyland to him and he was in a rush to get to it.

Meanwhile, the table behind Rabbit had been turned over. Another kid Rabbit's age sat directly behind Rabbit and across from him sat his mother, an attractive redhead with her hair in a messy bun. I was trying to be good, honestly I was—but I was so used to being me. She caught me noticing her and grinned. Rabbit, also observant, looked over his shoulder.

"She's pretty," he said, returning his attention to his placemat while we waited for the check—he'd started drawing in a landscape behind the car, with a curved orange road and green trees.

"Yeah, she is," I said.

"Not as pretty as my momma though."

"Definitely not," I agreed.

AFTER THAT, Happyland was ours. I followed him from game to game, helping him to win when he'd let me—unless he wanted to play against me, whereupon I'd put up a decent fight before 'losing' to him. I was particularly good at skee ball—and he really enjoyed accruing tickets.

"Hey, so how's Mark?" I asked, pitching the ball into one of the 50 point concentric rings again. "Is he a good guy?"

"I dunno," Rabbit said, from hovering over the vicinity of the next machine over's ticket extruder, trying to finagle another one out with his small fingers.

"Do you like him?"

"He's all right." He held up the free ticket he'd stolen with unabashed glee. "My best friend likes him."

"Yeah? Who's that?"

"Buster."

"What kind of name is Buster?"

"I dunno. He's imaginary."

"Does he know that?" I asked, and Rabbit snickered.

"That's what mom says."

"So, this Buster—does he have good taste in people?"

"I dunno."

"Does Buster like me?"

"Yeah."

"Then he must." I pitched in the last ball, and Rabbit carefully pulled off the twenty tickets we'd earned. "Ready to spend these and go home?" I'd reached the end of my cash on hand, and it was getting late.

"No!" he protested. "Not yet!"

"I'm all out of quarters, Rabbit," I said, ruffling his hair.

I could see his mind wildly searching for options. "There's a ball pit! The ball pit is free!" he said, grabbed my hand, and started running backwards.

"Only fifteen more minutes," I said, letting him pull me.

THERE WAS INDEED A BALL PIT, and while wild horses couldn't have gotten me inside of it, Rabbit was content to plunge in, leaving me with all his tickets to guard. I sat on one of the benches that lined the nearby wall, joining the other parental-inmates killing time, playing with their phones.

Are you done yet?

A text from Paco, from an hour ago. *Almost*, I texted back. *Just fifteen more minutes.*

There's no way to actually protect you here. Too many doors and only one of me.

We're fine, Paco. The most frightening thing here is whatever's in the bottom of the ball pit. How do they even clean those things? Do they even clean them? There could be a body in there, is what I'm saying.

I was interrupted from whatever Paco said next by the arrival of a lean tan woman with black hair in shining waves, black jeans, black low-cut top, and a push-up bra holding her breasts up for easy inspection. She looked over at me from where she'd sat down, clearly too close. "Are you as exhausted as I am?" she said, giving me a weary look.

"I don't know—I've only been here an hour and a half."

"Three hours. I got drunk, but now I'm sober again, and if I hear one more," she gestured back toward the cacophony of the arcade floor, rather than finish her sentence, "I'm going to shoot someone."

I laughed. "Which one is yours?" I asked, looking out into the sea of multicolored balls.

"Lexie—third from the left—Lexie, don't!" She shouted the last part louder, as Lexie proceeded to pitch a ball as hard as she could at the netting keeping the balls in. It bounced back, almost hitting another kid's face, and she laughed. "Sorry."

"It's all right—mine's Rabbit, back in the corner." He was making a row of red balls, then trying to create a pyramid.

"What an interesting name! What's it mean?"

"Uh." Truth was, I'd never asked Angela. When I'd met Rabbit, it'd just made sense. He'd always been small and a little too fast. "His mom picked it."

"Oh!" she said, then looked at me. "Is she here, too?"

The hunger lurched inside me again, same as it had at dinner for the redhead. "She is not." Nothing I could do about things tonight, but there was nothing wrong with keeping my options open for later. "I'm his uncle, by the way."

She smirked a little at me taking her bait. "I would've guessed that. You don't look anything like him. I bet he takes after his dad. Your...brother?" she tried.

"No—I'm related to his mom."

"Ahh. Faithful uncle, out on the town."

"Yeah, she's off on a date night and, well—you? You come here often?"

"Often enough to have the club card," she said with a chuckle. "And I'm on my own tonight too, if that's what you're asking."

And that's what I liked about moms. Once you got past the veneer of propriety, they didn't like to waste time. I gave her a wide smile, trying to envision a world in which I saddled Paco with both Rabbit and Lexie and took her back to my car. "I was —but...."

"Girlfriend?" she interrupted.

"No. I just can't be a bad example for him." I jerked my chin in Rabbit's direction.

She gave me a 'get-serious' look, subtly pushing her chest out and leaning forward. "Like that's ever stopped a man."

And I wasn't even one. But I'd made a promise—and Paco would never let me hear the end of it if I ditched Rabbit, besides. I inhaled and exhaled, standing before turning toward her. "You're pretty much exactly my type and I'd love to get your number for later—later on tonight, even. But for right now, I have to be good."

She stroked a hand through her hair and tossed it back, staring up at me with challenge in her eyes. "Good's overrated."

My eyebrows rose. I was so used to being the predator the experience reversed was novel. "What're you even suggesting?"

"I have my Lexie watch your Rabbit and you and I find somewhere accommodating. This place has got to have a broom closet. We're away ten minutes, tops." The hunger rose up inside of me like a separate beast, and it was *very* interested in her proposition. "I mean, I'm sure in better circumstances, we could manage things for longer—but when you're a parent, you catch as catch can." She stood up beside me, like I'd said yes and we were about to go somewhere. "I'm Nikki," she said, offering out a perfectly manicured hand, with nails I could already imagine clawing down my back when I put her on a wall.

"Jack," I said, reaching out to shake it.

A jolt of electricity passed between us—*no*—only me. I could tell by her triumphant expression that she thought nothing had changed.

But I'd felt like that before—when I'd touched Angela, a few nights ago. I didn't know what that meant—but something was not right, and I pulled back. "Numbers, maybe?"

"Really?" she said.

"Yeah—it's past our bedtime." I looked over my shoulder where Rabbit was now playing with Lexie, pitching balls with glee. "Rabbit! Time to go!"

"But Jackkkk," he started whining.

I turned to face him. "*We're going,*" I said, letting a hint of my whammy through. He started wading through the ball pit in response.

"What happened?" Nikki asked me, reaching out to rest her hand on my arm and drag it down, trying to slow me.

"Nothing," I said, stepping back and away toward Rabbit. When he got to the edge of the pit, I boosted him up and held him like a much smaller child. "It's past his bedtime, and we've got to go. Nice meeting you."

She pouted. "Nice meeting you, too."

We started walking toward the entrance and I didn't set Rabbit down. He knew something was wrong. "What's going on?"

"Nothing," I lied to him as well, pulling out my phone to text Paco: *Heading home.*

We stayed in the shadows in the entryway, waiting until we saw Paco's dark car circle near, then walked out under his watchful eyes.

"You're sure everything's okay?" Rabbit asked, after I'd installed him in my car, closing the door firmly behind him.

"Yeah. It's fine," I said, getting in the other side. "You had fun, didn't you?"

"I did! I didn't get to spend these, though," he said, shaking a fistful of tickets at me.

"Save them for next time, then."

"There's going to be a next time?" Rabbit asked, hope in his voice.

"Yeah. Swear." Hanging out with Rabbit wasn't so bad. And next time I'd have made sure to feed, plus we'd stay away from strangely electric women. I pulled out of the Happyland parking lot, with Paco's car right behind mine, not even pretending to hide. Why had Nikki felt like Angela? What could they possibly have in common? Was I a fool to let it spook me?

"I hope Lexie's there next time," Rabbit said.

"Why's that?" I asked, flipping on a turn signal.

"Because Buster really liked Fluffy."

"Fluffy who?"

"Lexie's imaginary friend."

I gave him side-eye. "Yeah? The two of them talk? Have a big conversation?"

"They don't talk, Jack," Rabbit said, with the exasperation of a child who knows he's being patronized. "They're doggies. It's like barks and feelings."

I inhaled to say something snarky but all that came out was, "Oh." And suddenly I didn't think I needed to have Rabbit touch silver anymore to prove anything.

CHAPTER SIXTEEN
JACK

We parked in the apartment's parking lot and Paco pulled up beside us. It was pushing ten-thirty, Rabbit's grandma was certainly back by now. Paco gave me a nod, which I returned, and Rabbit hopped out of the car none-the-wiser, bouncing excitedly across the parking lot.

"Wait up," I told him. He jumped up onto the curb and walked along it like it was a tightrope, until I caught up to him. "I hope you're tired. You've got to go to school tomorrow, right?"

"No, tomorrow's Saturday." *The things you lose track of when you spend half your life dead.*

"You still have your house key?"

Rabbit held it up like a trophy. "Yep!"

"Good." Because the last thing in the world I wanted to do was have to go back and fish it out of the ball pit.

One of the lights outside Angela's apartment was out. I felt sure it'd been working when we'd left.

"Can I do it?" he asked, when we got to his door.

"We could just ring the doorbell."

"I'm going to do it," he said, bringing the key out. It took his clumsy hands longer to fit it into the lock, and when he tried to turn it, it wouldn't budge.

"Need some help?" I asked, after watching him struggle.

"Yeah," he admitted, stepping back. My hand found the key in the semi-dark, and felt a pattern of scratches against the key-plate—and it was hard to turn now, I had to twist it slowly, afraid of breaking the key off in the lock.

I opened the door, pushing Rabbit back on instinct, as I realized the entire apartment was dark—and I could smell blood. A lot of it. Fresh and true.

"Fuck," I whispered.

"Don't cuss," Rabbit said, surely in imitation of his mother.

Without thinking, I grabbed him, and ran.

We flew to the end of the hall and I took the stairs two by two, Rabbit struggling all the while. "Put me down!"

"Stop it," I said, and shook him for emphasis. Parts of me I wanted to ignore forever said I could easily make him stop squirming with a bite.

I raced across the parking lot with him under one arm until we reached Paco's car, where Paco was already rolling the window down. "What's wrong?"

I was about to announce that someone was dead when I remembered who I was holding. I opened up the back of Paco's sedan and tossed Rabbit in back. "*Go to sleep, now,*" I growled. He landed, and whirled, almost clambering back out.

"*GO TO SLEEP,*" I commanded, with all of my will—and Rabbit slumped into the wheel well behind Paco's seat.

"What the fuck, Jack?" Paco growled.

"Get somewhere safe, fast, and call 911. I smelled blood—someone's dead up there."

Paco started. "Who?"

"Grandma, I'm afraid—if she's still alive, I'll see what I can do but," I quickly shook my head.

"You can't go back up there alone!" Paco's lips pulled into a thin line and his expression became determined.

"I'm not alone. Someone gave me a silver knife." I slammed the car door. As I ran back the way I'd come I heard Paco's car squeal out of the parking lot—and I was sure I saw someone peeking out from in-between Angela's blinds above.

THE DOOR WAS open like we'd left it, the scent of blood still wafting in the air. My eyes adjusted to the near dark instantly and I listened for any signs of human life, hisses of breath, the desperate thudding of a low-blooded heart—but nothing. And when I reached the living room, I knew why—Angela's mother was crumpled on the floor, her head at an odd angle, almost twisted off. *Bastards.*

I knelt down, the scent of blood an almost overwhelming temptation—except for the fact that it was cut with slightly sour dog.

I heard a rustle behind me, one any mortal would've missed, and it was hard not to whirl—but my advantage was that whichever Pack member stayed behind thought that I was human. I carefully knelt down as if considering the corpse.

The man behind me came up in an eager rush—I threw myself sideways and kicked out, catching his legs, sending him sprawling to the bloody ground for a moment before he bounced back up, trying to catch me before I could rise. I rolled sideways and lunged at him. He feinted and jumped behind the couch, and I realized I had another advantage as well—I was between him and the door.

He was one of the men I'd seen at the were-bar—the older seeming one, Daziel. "What the hell do you want with Angela?" I asked, matching each of his movements like a mirror, ready to stop his escape.

"This doesn't concern you—get the fuck out of the way." He

grabbed hold of the short side of the couch and hefted it—it went up and over lengthwise, clunking to lean against the wall, as he tried to run. I threw myself after him, taking him down by his legs. He kicked and caught me in my chest, and I felt ribs break and begin to instantly reknit. I yanked him back bodily, as he scrabbled at an end table, sending a lamp crashing to the ground.

"*Tell me!*" I compelled him, inching him back.

"It's the boy!" he shouted, then wriggled one leg free to kick at my jaw. My head snapped back, reeling, but I refused to let go of the other leg, so he redoubled over himself like a snake, coming to wrestle, wrapping both his hands around my throat.

Once again, I remembered pain. I punched him in his side, in his ribs and gut, but he held on, and I could feel my windpipe crunching —but I didn't really need to breathe. I scrabbled my knee up beside him, reached into my boot and freed the knife.

I plunged it into his side—I could feel it fight to get through the leather of his coat, but when it reached his flesh it made it part like warm butter. He howled and released me, arcing back, one hand instinctively going for his wounded side, the other out for balance and I—I sliced at it. The knife fell between his fingers, cleaving his ringfinger and pinkie right off.

His anger surged, I could feel it like an oncoming storm—but then sirens began wailing outside. He leapt and raced for the door, faster than I could react, as I heard boots stomping up the outside stairs.

I had just enough time to put the knife away and move to a kneel as the cops came in, guns and flashlights blazing. I could feel blood soaking in through the denim of my jeans—the werewolf's or Angela's mother, I didn't know—all I could think of was *water, water everywhere and not a drop to drink*—before I was tackled.

CHAPTER SEVENTEEN
ANGELA

Mark grinned at me as I returned to our booth and sat down. "You look happy." He'd watched the whole thing go down from a distance, and I had no idea what he was thinking.

"I got us invites. Room two-thirty-eight in ten."

One of his eyebrows arched. "You're sure she's not a pro?"

"Would it count less if she was?" I crossed my legs at the ankles demurely.

"Not in the least." He finished the last of his drink and set it down. "Now will you believe me that you're the most beautiful woman here?"

I grinned at him, beaming. "I'll give myself top ten, how's that?"

"Close enough."

Either of us could call it a night, now—I'd proved something silly to myself, there was no reason to push on, and yet…. "What's your word if I should call it off?"

He thought for a moment. "Rambunctious. And yours?"

"The same."

I was close enough to feel the heat radiating off of him, to hear his interest in the way his breath caught in his throat. I was almost positive that if I reached down to touch him through his slacks, I'd find him hard.

"What's she going to do to you?" he asked, his voice so low that I was the only one who could possibly hear it.

"That's the wrong question," I corrected him. "You should be asking what I'm going to do to her." I took his hand and stood back up.

TEN MINUTES later we were outside 'Christa's' door. Mark said, "Ladies first," and I lifted my hand to knock.

I rapped gently—there was still a chance that she'd just given me a room number to get away—but moments later she opened the door, wearing the same peach dress she'd been wearing at the club.

"Come on in, *Samantha*," she said, turning the name into a purr, before glancing at Mark. "Do you have a code name yet? No? Then I'm going to call you Thor—Thor, go sit in that chair."

We both walked into her room, where she'd taken a chair and placed it across from the bed facing the wall. Mark gave me a look, then did as he was told.

"I don't want to hear anything from you, Thor," Christa said as he sat down. "And no looking back. All you get to do is listen."

I could see Mark's jaw tense in profile. But he had a safeword—and her hand was trailing down my arm again, pulling me toward the bed.

I went with her. "There's no way this won't be awkward," I pre-apologized.

"Will it?" she asked, casting a sly glance toward Mark. "I don't know, I bet it's like riding a bike." She sat down, and I sat down beside her. "Too far," she complained, coming nearer. She twisted to face me, her eyes searching mine.

"How long has it been?" she asked, as her fingertips began to investigate the bottom of my skirt.

"Seven years. Almost eight." Every time Rabbit had a birthday, I thought about how Willa and her baby...the look on Christa's face as she read mine, went from inscrutable to kind. She raised her hand to my cheek and placed it against the line of my jaw.

"I'll be gentle then," she said, leaning in to kiss me.

All at once I remembered how kissing girls felt right. Her lips fit mine like they were twins, gentle and soft, as her tongue pushed out to meet mine. I tilted my head, closed my eyes, and gave myself over to the sensations. She was—this *was*—memories came rushing back, and a hunger I'd kept quiet for almost a decade roared.

"Yeah," she breathed, pulling back, sensing the change in me. I moved in to follow her, sliding my hand around her waist. We kissed again and again, the twine of our tongues urging our bodies to join them. We leaned close and, almost as one, fell back against the bed. My hands went for her hair to keep her mouth near mine while her hands roamed my body, making broad strokes over the stiff fabric of my dress, sending shivers down my spine. One of her legs tossed over me, her skirt rising high, as I sank one of my hands down to hold her ass while I pushed my hips towards hers.

"Mmm," she purred, rocking her hips in my time. Her hands circled my neck to fight the zipper that held my dress up, as I started pulling her dress up with eager palms. "Turn over," she commanded, unable to get hold of the zipper's tiny tab. I did as I was told, whirling right there against her. She lifted my hair up, kissed my neck, and then started to tug.

I could feel the fabric shift, revealing me, and heard her gasp. "Oh. That's lovely."

She'd found the largest of my many tattoos. After the roses that covered up my wolf-prints, and after Willa's willow—I'd kept with a greenery theme, like a modern-day Poison Ivy, and I had a peony at the nape of my neck. "I have a lot more," I warned her.

"I'm looking forward to finding them," she said—and then licked me. Goose bumps sprang up over my whole body. "Sensitive?"

"Very," I whispered.

"I'll remember that," she murmured, and kept pulling the zipper down. Each tattoo received its own moment of licking reverence, or biting, or the heat of her breath, one by one. My time with Gray had made me aware of how fragile life was, of how easily everything could be stripped away—and as if to fight that, I'd marked my history on myself, like I was a blank page. To a random observer, my back would look like a riotous English garden, covered in colorful blooms and blades of green. But I knew what each one stood for, a lily for my grandmother, a daffodil for my father, and a poppy for my grandfather and columbines, foxgloves and hollyhocks in-between —and nestled right behind my left shoulder, opposite my heart, a rabbit curled and sleeping in the grass.

Christa rose up, still fully clothed and straddling me as the zipper reached the end. "You're lovely," she said, with reverence.

I smiled and tucked my head down, suddenly shy. "Thank you."

She dismounted the bed and sidled the dress off, me helping her, well aware of the heat building between my thighs. I was embarrassed to be so eager, and yet how could I not be?

"Roll over, Samantha," she said, and I turned, hair spilling across my face. "Mmm, even more," she said, joining me on the bed again, moving to be above me on all fours. Her lips found my roses and tasted them. Mere inches away, caressed by her hair, my nipples went hard.

I reached up to touch her, to pull her to me, to try to get some traction on this ride—but she ignored me utterly, concentrating only on kissing every marked part of my body. From the roses to the vines that trailed them—for some reason getting thorns on me had seemed so necessary for protection years ago—to the willow on my hip—her lips found it and she was close, so close to the line where my underwear began and it was hard not to remember Willa kissing there, kissing all over me—my nearest hand went into her hair unbidden, and I didn't know if I was going to push her away or pull her closer.

"You okay?" she whispered, the words brushing against me.

"It's just," I began, my voice raw, and I saw Mark behind her, stirring in his seat in case I called this off. Christa looked at me, eyes full of concern—but I could see her breasts pushing forward in her dress and feel the heat of her breath on me. "It's been awhile is all."

"I can go slow."

I rolled my lips between my teeth, and then decided to be honest. "I'd rather you go faster."

She grinned. "Me too."

She took another salacious lick from the waistband of my underwear up to the bottom of my breast and then over it, circling my nipple, before standing up to shimmy out of her clothes. Her bra was the same color as the dress had been, her underwear just a little darker, and as I put my hands out for her she returned to the bed, pressing me back down.

Everything my hands had been denied earlier they now sought out—the smooth skin of her back, the softness of her breasts—her bra lasted only moments until it was off, revealing areolas the same sweet peach as her dress had been. I went for one with my mouth as her knee slid between my legs. Without thinking I ground against it, rocking myself against her as I sucked, nuzzling my face against her skin, loving the way her breath caught every time my tongue swiped across her nipples.

"Oh—that's so good," she purred, then turned her head in Mark's direction. "Are you listening, Thor?"

"Am I allowed to say if I am?" he asked in a rumble.

She laughed and pressed lower into me, so that we were skin to skin in so many places. Her hands found the waistline of my underwear and pushed—I wriggled to help her free me, then watched her free herself. She was sporting a Brazilian—I'd never seen someone with one in real life. "Come here," I whispered.

She knelt on the bed beside me, presenting herself. I leaned up on one arm to trace a curved path down her body, over her breast, her stomach, her hips, stroking lower—

"Here," she said, catching my hand and bringing it up again, taking the first two fingers into her mouth to get them wet. "Go." She spread her knees a little wider and I knew what she meant.

I didn't waste any of the precious fluid—I gently reached between her thighs while slicked with her spit, touching her soft folds. From where I was on the bed I could see the pink hood of her clit, tucked neatly between her labia majora. I worked my fingers back slowly, concentrating on the sensations for me and her, knowing she was watching me with her wide-eyes—and then I found the entrance of her pussy. She was already wet, and I wanted nothing more than to push a finger inside.

"Do it," she whispered, so I did, sliding a finger up, feeling the hot walls close in, soft and supple. She made a pleased sound, and I pushed in another, starting to stroke inside her the way Willa had sometimes stroked in me and, rubbing forward, and she made a much lower moan.

Empowered, I rose up, keeping my fingers still inside her, and started kissing wherever I could reach again, her neck, her throat, her breasts, while pulling inside her, calling her pussy to me. When my other hand rose up to pull her short hair back, setting her balance a little off, exposing more of her neck for me to lick up it she murmured, "You have done this before."

I didn't bother with an answer—I just pulled my fingers out a little and started circling her clit with her wetness. "I need to taste you."

I saw her chest rise then as her breath caught. She went down on her heels and then rolled back to lay against her bed, propped up on all the pillows. I lay on my stomach and followed her, crawling up between her legs, holding myself on my elbows so that she could see my cleavage and then lowered my mouth to dine.

My tongue slipped through to the places where fingers had just been, and I did everything that I remembered felt good, getting the tip of my tongue up under her hood so that I could roll my tongue against her clit as my lips sucked and pulled. She started making small noises for me, tiny gasps, high pitched whines—I knew she liked what I was doing, even before I slid my fingers back inside.

Her walls took them in and held them tight. I started rubbing again inside, like I was begging her to come to me—or for me.

"Ooh—yes, that—right there," she said, pressing her hips up higher with her feet. One of her hands was in my hair, the other avidly stroking one breast, pulling a nipple. Then her hand in my hair twisted, catching me. "Turn the chair around, Thor."

I stiffened—I'd been eating her out with abandon—I'd almost forgotten he was there.

"Keep going," she told me, letting my hair go, as I heard him resettle. I could almost feel his gaze on me, sliding over my back— and then up her stomach. "More," she begged, arcing her hips and— Mark had a safeword—and her pussy was *hot*—I redoubled my efforts.

Christa started thrashing on the bed, at first I thought for show, for Mark, but then the way she started and stopped, the sounds she made—I realized she almost wasn't in control. I rubbed harder, sucked harder, moaned myself to encourage her, delighted to re-experience this profound power over another woman. Her hips arced and shivered, and I felt her ass rock her beneath my mouth as her feet danced beside me. Waxed clean, I could see everything, taste everything, so easily—I spread her wide for me with one hand and sucked and rolled, rolled and sucked, she started making rising moans as I stroked her walls deep inside and then—

Her pussy clenched around me as her stomach curled and her hips rocked and she shamelessly shouted her orgasm out, coming around me, coming in front of me, coming *for* me. My mouth followed her hips through her spasms, still sucking, feeling the echoes of her orgasm try to pull my fingers in, until she made a final conquered sound. I moaned into her, carefully slid my fingers out, and kissed her pussy gently, before wiping my face clean on her thighs.

"Oh, Samantha," she purred, looking down at me, eyes glazed.

"That was good." She lazily gazed past me at Mark. "Wouldn't you agree, Thor?"

"I would have to," Mark said, his voice rough.

I didn't want to look back at him—I didn't want to feel guilty for anything I'd done. But I loved him and—I twisted to look over my shoulder, just in case. I should've trusted him and known better. The look he gave us both was smoldering—and his erection strained against his slacks. By now, he must be so hard, so tormented—I wanted to crawl over to him, unzip his slacks and unveil it, feel him tangle his hands in my hair and fuck my mouth until he came.

As if reading my mind, the corners of his lips quirked up into a grin. "Don't get distracted, darling."

"Definitely not," Christa answered, on my behalf. She swung one perfect leg over me to roll off the bed and went to stand by Mark. "I need some props—can I trouble you for your belt and tie?"

Mark took his tie off readily to hand over, but held back the belt. "If you hurt her," he threatened.

"I wouldn't dream of it," Christa promised, taking it from him, and returning to me. "This'll take some coordination, so be patient," she said—before tying Mark's tie around my left wrist. She fastened it under the bed, and did the same with the belt on the other side, until I was sprawled out on the bed with a foot of slack on either side, trapped between kneeling and lying face down, waiting to see what her next move would be.

She lay down beside me and snuggled underneath my arm, and I chose to lay down and put us body to body, so that my skin was against hers, even if I didn't have control of my hands. She started kissing me and I writhed, kissing her back avidly, longing to be free.

"See?" she said, bringing her unbound hand up to pull at my nipple. All I could do was watch as she lowered her mouth down to kiss it, wait for the fire to spring up from where her mouth touched and feel it jolt straight down to my hips. "Mmm," she said, like I tasted good, and took another lick.

I roiled against my ties, trying to present more of myself to her, wanting to take more of her for mine—but she kept kissing, my neck, my ribs, my breast, in huge circles that always came back to my nipples and then she started gently using teeth and—I cried out in surprise and in longing, and Mark almost came out of his chair, I heard it.

"Don't hurt her."

Christa chuckled against me. "I'm only hurting her the way she wants to be hurt." She reached down and grabbed my hips, bringing her leg between them which I accepted readily to grind against.

After already fucking her, and my own fire so thoroughly stoked —my lips sought hers out, as if I could beg her to take care of me with my kiss. Our lips met and she rolled herself underneath me, so that we were hip to hip, breasts to breasts, kissing hard, legs tangled as we twined. If she would just stay still—if she would just keep touching me—her lips reached my ear. "Let's give your man the full show."

I didn't know what that meant, but all I could do was to agree. Her hands reached down, grabbed hold of my ass, and pulled me wide, as if presenting my pussy to him.

"See how wet I made your girl?" she asked, looking down the length of the bed at him, behind me.

I froze, not knowing how Mark would respond, until I heard his basso: "You should see her when she comes."

Christa laughed, still kissing me. "I intend to," she said, and then rolled out from under me. "Up on your knees," she commanded, and I did as I was told. "Spread them," she said, and I did that too.

With cat-like grace, she slid herself under me again—only this time on her back, with her head between my legs pointing towards Mark. We were body to body again, only this time reversed, so that there was almost no way I could support myself up off of her. Her hands slid between us, to stroke at my breasts, which were pressed against her hips, the nipples barely poking out on each side.

And of course from here—her pussy. Right in front of me again, waxed clean—without thinking I lowered my head again to lick it.

"Yes," she hissed, pinching both of my nipples hard—before letting go and wrapping her hands around my hips and ass to call my pussy to her. My knees slid wider, until I could feel her breath and then—

Her tongue, at long last. Fingers pulled me open, exposing my clit, and I felt her lips fasten on.

"Oh God," I murmured into her, and I felt her laugh. She kissed my clit, working at it with her lips and tongue while I went perfectly still to let her. I knew my ass was arched back, I knew Mark could see everything, but I didn't care—I started to grind my hips into her without shame. She purred, and then brought both of her hands up to push fingers in.

She kept me wide, stretching my pussy from one side then the other, stirring her fingers inside, first one, then two, then three. I moaned, feeling stretched and hungry.

In return, I lapped at her eagerly. I could only take what she was willing to give me, since I could barely brace my arms, but I tried; running my tongue over any part of her I could get, her thrusting up at me as I licked down. She was like salt and earth and musk and part of me wondered how I'd possibly been able to stand it so long, living without a woman's taste in my mouth.

She gasped, reaching down to hold my head at a certain spot, and I kept doing what I'd been doing with my tongue. "Oh—yeah—right there," she moaned, arching her hips up and spreading her legs wide. I kept going, I knew how to do what I was told, running my tongue against her clit's side, back and forth, up and down.

"Oh my God," she whispered, letting go of my head and trusting me, just as her other hand left my pussy and started tracing up.

I heard Mark gasp as I felt what she was doing—pushing a finger, slicked with my juices, into my ass.

I had never—and yet—I cried out into her as she kept sucking me, not going deep, just holding space there. All new nerves sang that it was different—but that everything still felt *good*.

And then she brought her other hand to bear, filling my pussy back up, and it was hard to concentrate. I wanted to make her come again, but I was losing concentration, and then I heard Mark give a low order. "Fuck her good for me."

Yes. Of course. That was why we were here—I focused and redoubled my efforts, as Christa started to moan breathlessly into my cunt. She was so close, I could tell by the way her hips moved and her legs trembled.

"Oh God," she groaned, making it reverberate into me. "Oh my God—oh my God!" her voice rose in pitch, until she started rhythmically thrashing below me, coming once again. I followed her with my mouth, seeing her through, incredibly turned on, until she reached a hand down to pull on my hair to stop me.

I lifted my head up, my mouth and chin dripping with her juices, panting, as I heard Mark speak again. "Fuck her harder."

I blinked, endorphin-dazed and not entirely understanding. I'd just made Christa come, what could possibly be left?

Then I realized he was talking *to* her. Not me. And never had been.

Christa tsked, pushing my hips up enough for her to talk. "You're not the boss of me, Thor," she taunted.

"No," he agreed. "But I am the boss of *her*," he said, and I felt a deep shudder of ownership, "and I want her to come so hard they can hear it on the next three floors." I could feel my skin flushing red at the thought of it, even as at the same time, it felt like a command.

Christa laughed, and took it like a challenge. She dragged my hips back to her and started working her magic with her hands. I was revved up in an instant, feeling taken every which way, and knowing that Mark was watching—*everything*—seeing me like this—spread wide—taken—helpless—I knew without looking that he was rock hard and that after this my man—my *mate*—was going to give me the fucking of a lifetime. Christa's tongue pulled against my clit as her gathered fingers shoved into my pussy and her solo-finger in my ass went deeper, and everything ignited all at once.

I shouted a howl, ground my hips down, and both heard and felt her purring as she made me come, while all of me was on display for him.

I thrashed against her and the bed like I was possessed as my orgasm wracked through me, curling me up as I screamed and kept screaming until it was through. Only Christa's wisdom at covering her teeth with her lips stopped me from getting cut. I collapsed against her, gasping, and only then did I feel the delicious sensation of her pulling her finger in my asshole out.

She swatted my hips with one hand. I shifted to release her as she laughed, far more mobile than I felt, moving by the bed to stand.

"Wow," she said, undoing the ties that held me at the bedframe. "Thor wasn't wrong. You are a screamer."

"When I get the chance to be," I said, lifting up.

"My goodness," she went on, holding up his belt. I'd cracked the leather, and the edges of his tie were frayed. My wolf's strength, not mine. Christa didn't untie my wrists, instead she presented the tie and belt to Mark like reins. "She's all yours again."

"Thanks," he said, standing up readily. He looked like he wanted to tear me up, in a good way—not angry, just intensely, deeply, turned on—and it was easy to see his cock at attention, tenting his slacks.

"I'm going to go take a long hot shower," Christa said, looking at me. "You're welcome to stay—but Thor, not so much." Then she went into the bathroom and closed the door behind her. I watched her go with a sense of longing and awe.

And just like that, a door that'd been long closed in my life had been blown wide open.

Mark let go of the ties to pick my dress up, and held it out to me. I took it from him. "Thank you," I said, earnestly. Not just for the dress, but for so much more.

CHAPTER EIGHTEEN
ANGELA

I n the end, Mark had to help me get dressed as the water started running in Christa's shower. I was feeling too many emotions—elation, surprise, confusion, fear—while Mark went so quiet I didn't want to ask him why, suddenly afraid I wouldn't like the answer.

After my dress was on, I held my hands out to be freed. He surveyed the damage I'd done to his belongings, and tsked, tucking them into pockets without putting them back on. We left her room and walked back to the elevators, through the casino, I thought back to his car, but he detoured us, as if we were going back to the club.

"Mark?" I finally dared to ask him, as got into the VIP elevator again. He keyed in a button, it rose—and then he hit a black button, stopping it. "Mark—what?"

"You're so fucking beautiful, Angela—and you're so beautiful when you fuck, do you know that?" I didn't know how to answer as he went on. "I need you. Now."

I knew what he meant, but I looked over my shoulder, at the casino floor, and panicked. "But everyone—"

"One way glass, I promise," he said, his hands already undoing his slacks. The hard on I knew had been waiting for me all this time thrust out just as I fell to my knees and kissed the tip of it slowly, like I was kissing him.

"Oh God, Angela—oh God," he breathed. We were close enough to the glass wall that he could put both his hands on it as he pushed toward me, begging me to take more in. So much precum, he must've been aching. I brought a hand up to rub his balls as I started sucking on his head. "Yeah," he said, with a shudder.

I tongued the bottom of his shaft how I knew he liked, and wondered—after watching all of that—what he needed to be satisfied. I worked my lips down his ramrod cock like it was a ticking time-bomb, waiting to explode. When it didn't, I started going faster, sucking with more force. How hard it must've been to watch me fuck and get fucked, and not be inside me—to be even maybe a little worried I was leaving him for her. I tried to suck any residual fear out of him, showing him how much I loved him now on my knees in this elevator, a whole casino floor outside, seemingly watching on.

He brought one hand down to run through my hair and pull me off of him. "More," he demanded, and I wanted to give it to him. I stood up as his hands moved to help me, and turned around quickly —I barely had time to brace against the glass before he'd pulled up my skirt and pulled my panties aside.

I was so wet he slid in fast, filling me all at once—I grunted and he moaned. "God, yes," he breathed. "Your pussy feels like home."

This was what my wolf wanted—what she'd been waiting for—we pressed back against the glass with our hands and bent over. With the extra height our heels gave us we were aligned perfectly.

"Angela," he said appreciatively—then stepped up so he was right behind us, cock in to the hilt, like we were one.

We stayed there for a long moment, just feeling each other, me stretched out, him stretching me, until I couldn't help but move a little and then he started to thrust and—his hands found the zipper at the back of my dress, opening it up so he could reach in and grab me. And it was like my nipples, already sensitive after

Christa, were on fire, everything he did to them covered me in electricity.

He started fucking me then, using my breasts for leverage, pulling me toward him as he pushed himself in. My jaw was dropped and I was panting and thirty-feet below us no one was the wiser, tourists walking around, drinking, talking, spending money. Suddenly I wished the glass were see through—I wanted everyone to know I was being taken by my man—and Mark's hands went to my hips.

"Angela," he warned me as his cock dove in—he started taking me roughly, like he had to mark his space in me all over again, he needed me right in this instant, all of me, wrapped around all of him —I knew he was getting close, I could hear it in his breathing and feel it in his cock. "Angela!" he shouted, claiming me at full volume, his cock twitching up as his hips spasmed. The glass was not soundproof—at him shouting, several of the people on the floor looked up. "Angela!" he shouted again, not caring, then turning it into a savage growl.

He fucked me through his orgasm, giving me every last drop of his load, until he pulled back. I held myself up on the wall, panting, absolutely sure I was full of cum.

Mark reached into his pocket for his phone and made a call before I could object. Hopefully telling them to erase the security tapes, although I almost liked the idea of some bored security guard covertly jerking off to me getting fucked. I dared to stand up as Mark put his phone away, and felt his leftover heat swell and leak between my thighs. He hit a code on the elevator door and I laughed.

"I can't go back to the club like this, Mark." I took his free hand and pulled it between my thighs so he would know the state he'd left me in. He gave me a sly grin and chuckled.

"Who said anything about the club?" he said, as the elevator rose higher.

THE ELEVATOR DOORS opened on I didn't know what floor, but it took us over a minute to get up there—long enough for me to push down my skirt and for Mark to help me with my zipper. The doors to the rooms were wideset, so I knew we were on a penthouse level floor, because each of them needed space for several rooms inside, for crazy things like nannies and butlers.

I felt a little out of place walking beside him in the hall. "Who'd you kick out this time?" I asked, remembering our night after the restaurant.

"No one—some ultra-high roller will just have to get comped on a lower floor." He waved his key in front of a door, and I saw a green flash as I heard the lock unlatch. "Go on—go in," he said, and I opened it up. It was as nice as the other room we'd been in but the lay-out was different—the wall that showcased the entire Strip was dominated by a deep hot tub that was already full and running.

"Really?" I said, asking him.

He grinned at me. "This is the honeymoon suite," he said, already shucking off his clothes.

"That's ridiculous!"

"Isn't it though?" he was three buttons down his shirt and he paused. "I like being ridiculous with you. Almost as much as I enjoy watching you get terrorized by lesbians."

"Technically, the terrorizing was mutual, and I liked it."

His hands on the next button down paused. "I know. That's what made it so hot."

I took off my shoes and kicked off my useless underwear. "Were you worried at all?"

"Of course. Who wouldn't be worried about losing you? But I'm a big enough man to know that if one night with another woman makes you leave, you were never really mine."

I managed to catch my own zipper and pull my dress off, standing naked on the tile. His shirt was off, and his slacks were on their way, after he kicked off his shoes. "You know what made me come so hard at the end there, with her?"

He freed himself from his last sock. "What?"

"The thought of you fucking the shit out of me, afterwards."

Mark grinned. "We'll get to that—but first things first," he said, walking over to the tub to stand inside it, offering a hand out.

I got in much less gracefully, it was easier when you were tall, but then we were both in the water safely. He lowered himself first, and I sank into his lap, fitting against him, the water barely covering my breasts. His arms wrapped around me, his chin against my forehead, my body giving into the water's heat and to him. We sat there, quiet and calm, staring out at the Strip, and for the first time in a long time I felt completely relaxed. "This is nice," I whispered, not wanting to break the mood.

He kissed my forehead. "I know." But then he picked us up and started to turn us and I knew some new good thing was coming—and suddenly I was hungry again, for whatever he had in mind—my wolf was always ready for her mate.

Mark hit a button on the tub's edge, and gentle jets started to spray beneath the water's surface. Then he moved us, pulling himself into the center of the tub, taking us with him, and spreading our legs wide.

A jet swirled and—I gasped.

"Uh huh," he agreed, pushing me closer, one arm under my breasts, the other keeping one thigh out wide. "Just...."

"Oh," I said, as the water raced over me again. Like the tongue of a mermaid, strong and wet. "Oh," I gasped again.

His face nuzzled against mine and he whispered in my ear. "I want you to come for me Angela." The water raced, flicking under the hood of my clit, enveloping it before racing away again. "There's nothing in the world I like better than making you feel good."

My breath caught and he pushed me in, so that the jet hit me harder. It was like a metronome, just long enough to be torturous between each stroke. "More?" I begged. His hand splashed out of the water and changed the setting, speeding it up and—

"Ohh...." It was double time now—doubly good, doubly satisfying. I arched my hips up as he pressed his hand between my legs to spread my pussy wide and—I bent my head against his, breathing.

"That's so good," he said, encouraging me. "Keep going."

I gave myself up, rocking my head back, letting the water take me. The jets spun so that just as one finished another started, it went from one to a dozen mermaids licking me and if I tilted my hips right it was like one deliciously continuous stream.

"You're so close," he said, feeling me tense. "Come for me, come for me, come for me," he whispered—and I did, rocking up. My body thrashed in the water as he held me tight, keeping the jets aimed right at my clit until I squirmed away, panting, all my hair wet. He held me tight then, curled up in a ball in his lap.

"Are you good?" he asked. I nodded against him. "Good," he said, licking up the shell of my ear. "Then—again."

"Oh God," I whispered, as he pushed my hips forward, but I didn't stop him.

MARK MADE me use the jets until I was a wreck. All the cum he'd put into me had definitely been washed away by the tub and my clit was almost sore from overuse. At the end, he'd taken me into his arms with a towel and stood, holding me like he really was Thor, and carried me into the next room for the bed.

He lay me down gently, dried himself off, and then joined me, laying himself alongside me. I had no idea what was coming next, but could already feel myself regrouping. For his part, he looked like he had something important to say, so I reached over to trace the outline of his lips. "What're you thinking?"

"That I love you."

I pulled my hand back, as if the words burned. No one I wasn't related to had told me they loved me in years. And here was this perfect, exceptional man, offering his love to me—and worse yet, I knew I loved him back.

But was it fair for me to let him love me, when he didn't really know what I was?

I reached back out for his lips carefully pressing them with my fingertips so he wouldn't protest what I was going to say next.

"Mark—I," I started, and I saw his face light up, and then his phone rang. He groaned.

"Ignore that—keep talking," he said, with hope in his eyes.

I wanted too—but it was hard as we both waited for whoever was calling him to go to voicemail. I nervously laughed and grinned and the second his phone stopped he leaned forward again. "Go on?"

I regathered myself, inhaling to tell him, *I'm a werewolf, no, really* —and then my phone started ringing. Mark could ignore his, but I was a mom—I swung my legs off the bed and lunged for my purse. As I picked up mine, his began to ring again. We looked at each other, and this time he dove for his phone.

CHAPTER NINETEEN
JACK

After the cops arrived, all of my protests fell on deaf ears. I was lucky not to be shot on sight, honestly—and lucky that I'd managed to get a souvenir—Daziel's fingers proved he'd been there, and that we'd fought, seeing as everyone thought it was unlikely that a woman with a bad hip pushing seventy had managed to move a couch prior to her imminent demise. But that didn't stop me from being taken downtown.

I kept repeating my story, the exact same story, to a slew of different cops. It would've been easier to prove if I looked like I'd been in a struggle, but other than being a little disheveled, I'd healed too fast to let on. Then again that was better than healing slowly here, right in front of their faces.

I knew my story would check out—they'd confirm it with Paco or Angela eventually—but seeing as I wasn't on any files and I didn't have any identification, they were more interested in me than I liked, taking away my phone and knife. I managed to use my whammy when they were taking my fingerprints, so they didn't notice they were blurry smudges, but after that there were too many people around—and I didn't dare do it anywhere I might be taped. Over the next several hours I was in rooms with assorted officers, one, two, even three, or left completely alone, presumably to reconsider my story. The only constant was the omnipresent sound of clocks slowly ticking down toward dawn.

When I wasn't being interrogated or afraid of dying in public, I was worried about Rabbit. Where had Paco taken him and was it really safe? I was glad I'd gotten the chance to warn Paco about the Pack being werewolves—but if anything happened Rabbit or him—

"You look a little tense," the next officer who came in said, in a congenial good-cop way.

It was all I could do not to strangle him. "I just found a body, so, yeah."

I WAS HOPING FOR ANGELA, but who I wound up getting was Mark. He walked into the room they were keeping me in sometime after five a.m., looking haggard, flanked by two cops—I instantly stood, and the cops were instantly on guard.

"Angela? Rabbit?" I asked Mark, turning their names into questions.

"They're safe," he said guardedly. "Paco said I needed to come vouch for you. How do you even know him?"

"Why is he watching her?"

"He asked you a question," the officer on the right said, willing to see how this played out.

I sighed. "We've known each other for a long time. I spotted him there the other night when I dropped by to ask about when Dark Ink was opening back up."

"You spend a lot of time outside your boss's apartment complex?" asked Officer Left.

"I'm her nightshift employee. She knows me—I was babysitting her son." I gave Mark a look. I wasn't going to beg, but he damn well knew the truth. "I've worked for her, for what, five years?"

"And yet you don't have a license to give tattoos in this state," said Officer Right.

The three of them were a wall. "What the fuck is happening here? I did the right thing—I protected Rabbit, and I gave you assholes your only clue. I'm still wearing clothes that have some stranger's blood on them and blood from my friend's mom—my night has been the definition of fucked up." I stared, challenging them to doubt me. "Can I please go home now?" I spoke slowly, making each word into a sentence.

The line of Mark's jaw tightened and I realized as shitty as things had been for me, his night had been far worse. I fell back into the chair behind me. "I'm sorry about Martha, and I'm glad Angie's safe. Just keep her safe, okay? Whoever the fuck those guys were, they weren't messing around."

For a moment silence reigned and then Mark shook his head. "He's not your guy," he told the cops."

"Are you sure? I mean, look at him," Officer Right said.

Mark stiffened and turned and for a moment I had some idea of how he'd act in court. "If you're implying that someone with tattoos is always a suspect, then you're also implicating my girlfriend."

While Mark's attention was occupied with Officer Right, Officer Left shrugged one shoulder like, *Possibly*.

"Let him go."

"Are you offering to represent him?"

"I don't need to, because you're not keeping him anymore. Give him his stuff back, and a taxi voucher."

Officer Left decided to pull Mark's chain. "You want him to leave so bad, your law firm can pay."

Mark bristled even further—and I realized he had some sort of relationship with these men, they were definitely not strangers. Just what kind of lawyering did he do? I'd never thought to ask.

"Here," Mark went for his wallet and pulled out a twenty.

I waved his offer away. "I'm good."

"Your wallet's empty," Officer Right pointed out.

"Last I checked, being broke in Vegas wasn't a crime," Mark said.

Which was technically true, but largely depended on what neighborhood you were in and how well you fit in there. I snorted. "If I can get my things back, I'm set, thanks," I said, as calmly as possible.

Mark nodded curtly. "Officers?" he said, pressing them to do their jobs, and then left like someone who was used to being obeyed. I moved to follow him, and they blocked my path quickly.

"I know my rights," I said, suddenly regretting calling them assholes earlier, no matter how good it'd felt at the time.

Officer Left gave me a shit-eating grin. "Aw, come on, just a few more questions."

Officer Right, agreed. "Yeah. I think you need to tell us everything you know about the Pack."

By the time they were convinced I didn't know anything and stopped holding me just to piss me and/or Mark off, it was perilously close to dawn. I had to fight not to run from the precinct—and as you might imagine, there weren't many cabs trolling nearby. By the time I'd hailed one and had whammied the driver to take me home I was sliding down in the back seat, half to hide from the rising sun, half because I could feel myself dying inside.

"Hurry," I implored him, whammying him shamelessly.

He started to ignore traffic laws and pulled me into my apartment complex at full speed, his cab rattling over speed bumps, until he screeched to a halt—on the wrong side.

"Around—the back," I gasped, and he went hurtling around—almost hitting a parking car.

I lurched out of the cab the second he parked again, shaking. Only sheer willpower kept me going—my door wasn't that far—and if I got under the awning I'd be safe from the sun....

"Hey!" a voice shouted behind me. Likely to tell off the cabbie—

and I heard the sound of feet running up behind me. *Keep going, Jack —just keep going—*

"Hey," the voice repeated, much nearer and more kindly than the cabbie deserved. "Are you okay?" A man loomed into vision. Florida —*Zach*—him and all his young muscles and ability to withstand daylight. "Whoa there. Are you all right?"

"No—I need to sleep this off," I said, slurring, as his arm wrapped around me and came up underneath my armpit. It was bright out, brighter than I'd seen in years. "Please—apartment thirty-six," I whispered, handing him my keys.

"Of course," he said—just as my vision went black.

CHAPTER TWENTY
ANGELA

My apartment smelled like my mother.

Not the normal smells of her, her skin, the body powder she used after she showered, the scent of her shampoo in her hair— no, it smelled like all the dark and unknowable parts of her, her blood, her piss, her shit, her fear. Inside me my wolf roiled in anger, in a way I was not allowed, pacing, growling, ready to lurch out and fight anyone, and me ready to let her—and we weren't even all the way inside yet.

"Are you sure you want to do this?" Mark's man, Paco, had come on again around seven p.m. that night and hadn't left me alone since, while Mark was off 'working.'

On saving me.

"We just need some things," I said. *And I have to see.* I left that part unspoken. But how could I not bear witness to the place where my mother'd died?

Especially when she'd died because of me?

He looked me over and then relented, letting me walk past him, through the kitchen, into the rest of the house. There were still pieces of police tape fluttering behind us on the door, all the doorjambs were dusted with black powder for lifting fingerprints, and little evidence markers were tented up by the most ominous bloodstains. My couch'd been flipped for some reason, who knew why, and just past it was the largest stain of all.

I knew it'd been hers.

They'd made me identify her body in the morgue, and by then they'd already collected their evidence and washed away the signs of her death—made her look as peaceful as possible for my sake. But I knew her—there was no way she'd gone down without a fight, for all her age and frailty, and this stain was from that struggle—the last few moments of her life.

I went down on my heels and reached out without thinking, and Paco rested his hand on my shoulder to stop me. "Don't," he counseled, in a gentle tone.

"Why not?"

"Trust me, the image here will stay with you long enough. You don't need to think about touching her blood every time you see your hand."

Wise, and true. I stayed there quiet for as long as I could, absorbing the horror before standing again.

"You said you needed to get some things, right?" Paco said, giving a pointed look to the duffle bag slung over my shoulder.

I nodded, and made to head up the stairs.

My room looked like a tornado had hit it. The mirror had been shattered, there were shards of glass everywhere—my counters had been swept free of knickknacks, mementos, and jewelry, the memories of a lifetime, sprawled upon the floor, the painting Jack had done of Rabbit torn in two. I held myself, surveying the damage. This was why I wore tattoos—no one could ever take them away from me.

What flower would I choose for my own mother?

A wave of regret pulsed through me, and Paco stepped closer, to catch me in case I fell. We both heard someone enter the apartment below us—the door was being guarded by police, but that didn't stop us both from tensing, until we heard the static-y garble of police radio chatter. I'd been given special permission to come back here, via strings Mark had pulled, but it could be revoked at any time and if I didn't pack now—I stomped over to my dresser and opened drawers, throwing their contents into the duffle bag. At the bottom of my underwear drawer, I found one of my emergency bottles of colloidal silver. I didn't need it anymore, I didn't think, but Rabbit—I shoved it into the bag, hoping Paco hadn't seen, or that he'd be smart enough not to ask. After that I went back into the hallway, and Paco followed me into Rabbit's room.

His room they'd left alone. They didn't want to hurt him—only to scare me into giving him up. *And to think at one point in time I'd thought Gray loved me.* I walked over to Rabbit's dresser and took more care packing, pulling out complete outfits for him, and choosing a few favorite toys, anything that would give him some semblance of normalcy. The sound of police chatter neared, and I knew Paco was putting himself between me and the door, as a detective arrived.

"We'll be done in a minute, officer," Paco said, addressing the man, without changing his position.

"I'd like to have a word with you," he said, angling around Paco as I ignored him. I needed to find the last Dino-blaster for Rabbit—there were four in the set, and if he'd ever put his toys back where they belonged....

Paco answered for me. "You can arrange that through her lawyer."

"It's good to see you again, Miss Roberts," said a distantly familiar voice. I stopped what I was doing, elbow deep in a jumble of toys.

"Her name is Wilshire," Paco growled, falling into defensive mode, ready to reach for his holstered weapon as I turned around.

"Officer," I said, quietly. The one and only time I'd used a fake name in my entire life was when I'd turned that woman's skull in to the police, years ago. I'd chosen my mother's maiden name in my panic.

"Paul Derizzio—remember me?" He came forward with his hand out, and then looked to Paco. "I'm going to need a moment alone with her."

Paco said nothing, just gave the man a dry look, and didn't move.

"It's okay," I said, coming up behind him. "Really."

"Nothing personal Miss Wilshire, but you're not really in charge here."

I stepped between the men and straightened my shoulders. "Paul's an old personal friend. He would never hurt me."

Paco clearly didn't believe me, but there were more cops downstairs, we were far outnumbered. He fished in his pocket and then shook Paul's still extended hand—satisfying himself that the cop was congenial perhaps?—and then moved aside. "I'll be outside the door."

Derizzio looked at his hand oddly, then wiped it on his leg once we were alone—and stepped back to close the door behind Paco. "Miss Wilshire? It's been awhile," he said.

"You can call me Angela—and it has been." I never got the chance to tell him how much I appreciated his discretion all those years ago, when he could've easily taken me in alongside Gray. "Thank you."

"No, thank you. You made my career. I'm a lieutenant now." He crossed the room to sit on Rabbit's bed, and patted the bed beside him for me. He was older now, soft gray dappling his temples. "I only needed that skull to get a warrant, and afterward—I said you were some drifter. You looked worse for the wear on the tapes from all the rain, and honestly, no one cared—Gray's lawyer argued that the skull was a set-up, but there was no denying the other bodies that we found."

I joined him on the bed, an arm's length down. "How many graves were there?"

"Eight bodies, plus some miscellaneous parts." He shrugged a shoulder, not being casual so much as inured to horror. "I've spent the past seven years wondering if I did the right thing that morning, not turning you in. I didn't know if you'd gone to ground, or if they'd found a different graveyard for you."

"I only moved back in with my parents and had a normal life."

"And a child, I see," he said, looking around at Rabbit's room.

"Yeah." It'd taken me so long to paint Rabbit's room for him—and now he'd never see it again. Or his grandma. I was taken aback by a fresh wave of pain, and somewhere inside me my wolf howled.

"I know you're grieving, but I have to ask—is the murder of your mother related to you or the Pack?"

I clenched my jaw and shook my head. "No."

"And this is a random act of senseless violence?" he pressed on.

"It must be," I whispered.

"Even though you've got the best bodyguards Carrera Law can buy?" He shifted on the bed to face me. "I know you don't really know me, Miss Wilshire, but I have your best interests at heart."

"Thank you, but—"

"You and your son need to be under round the clock police protection," he interrupted.

I stood and started walking toward the door. "What I need is to be nearer to my son right now—he cried himself to sleep last night, and if I'm not there when he wakes up...."

"Turn off the light," he said.

I blinked. "What?"

"Turn off the light," Derizzio he repeated, contemplating me from the bed. I sidled against the door, confident Paco was listening in on the other side. "Please, Angela."

My hand found the light switch and flipped it off. Lieutenant Derizzio pulled out a UV light of some sort and flashed it on the far wall—illuminating the clear outline of a rabbit. It took up the entire wall—I couldn't see it earlier, painted on the black. It'd traced over the edges of a painted supernova though, and that's what the officer had seen.

"It's in blood. Does that mean anything to you?" he asked.

They'd painted in his room in my mother's blood. A warning—and a promise to me that they would take him.

I was frozen with the horror of it all—and *she* took her chance. My wolf shifted forward, occupying me, with a mother's fury and a daughter's pain. I almost said things in her language, barks and growls, as it was I fell to the floor, feeling her shape make my bones start to bend.

"Angela?" Paco said, coming into the room at once, the door hitting me—the pain of that, and the flash as he hit the switch and the lights came back on—and the way his gun was pointed at Derizzio's head—the Lieutenant calmly held his hands up as I regathered myself, with Paco hunched over me, waiting for an attack.

"I'm all right."

"For now," Derizzio said. "But the forces after you," he began, as I started desperately pawing through my bag, "there's no way you can stop them. And no way you can pay enough people to protect you like I will—do you want to be at the mercy of your new boyfriend besides? How long can his patience—and bank account—last? Do you have any idea how expensive good help is these days?"

"With all due respect officer, shut up," Paco growled.

I found what I was looking for—the bottle of colloidal silver. I uncapped it and took a swig quickly, feeling it burn the entire length of my throat and fall into my stomach like poison. Everything that was wolf-like inside me ran away, leaving me, an exhausted woman in the depths of her grief, crumpled on the floor.

I started crying and I didn't stop until Paco had herded me into his car.

CHAPTER TWENTY-ONE
JACK

I woke up in a box. My box. No sounds of Sugar outside. I didn't positively know where my box was—but there was no sensation of movement, like I was inside a truck somewhere, being carted off to Area 51 or a Mexican circus.

I pushed the lid back, slowly, relieved to see my own bedroom outside—and the door, closed. How had I gotten here? What had Zach seen? I was still wearing the clothes I'd had on yesterday, down to my boots, he hadn't tried to undress me for bed in the least.

I opened the door and walked out into my living room—and found Zach, snoring on my couch, with Sugar snuggled into a furball on the center of his chest. She lifted her head, gave me a baleful glare, and then returned to ignoring me. I could see a full bowl of food for her on the floor of my kitchen, and the signs that Zach'd made himself a PB&J on the countertop.

I shook my head to all of that, and went into the bathroom to hop in the shower.

Surely Zach would wake up while I was in here, and realize his nurse duty was done and leave. Surely. I didn't want to have to roust him, and I certainly didn't want to answer any questions—but I listened for the sound of the front door and didn't hear it my entire shower. I got out, kicked my old clothes aside, tied a towel around my waist and braced.

Zach was sitting on my couch, petting Sugar with one hand while he ate a fresh sandwich with the other. He looked me up and down, and then made an effort to keep his eyes on my face. "Hey," he said, companionably, like he hadn't seen me die.

"Hey," I said back. "Thanks."

"You're welcome." He took another bite of his sandwich and chewed, contemplatively. "Are you...better?"

I tilted my head like that was a strange question. "Yeah. Why do you ask?"

His expression clouded. "So you probably don't remember."

Oh God. "Nope."

"You made me bring you into here, and then take you into your bedroom, and then you tried to pull me into that box after you and then you passed out. Hard."

I laughed it off, hoping he would too, trying not to think about what my hunger might've done to him unguarded. "Yeah? I'm sorry. Some nights are like that, you know?"

He gave Sugar a final pat, finished his sandwich and stood. "So... are you some kind of magician?"

I winced. "Why do you ask?"

"You sleep in a box. That's sort of quirky. And you have a white cat, maybe instead of a white rabbit? And—you have a lot of tattoos." His eyes flickered over my arms and chest. "Now that I can see them all, that is."

"If having tattoos was the only requirement for magician-hood, I know a ton of bikers who can float cars." I snorted. "Look, Zach, I appreciate you taking care of me this morning, but I'm fine now, so you can go home."

"Are you sure you're fine? Because you sleep like the dead."

I weighed that phrase for all its possible shades of meaning. If he'd been being literal, I would've whammied him to forget he'd ever known me, right then and there. But the goofy, slightly hopeful expression that followed it made it clear that he was trying to make a joke—and find a way to spend more time with me. "Yeah, I'm sure."

I took a few steps back so that he'd have a clear path through my living room to the front door, while he seemed to hesitate. His hair was tousled from sleeping on my couch, and his uniform was as rumpled as my own clothes had been, and he radiated a kind of pleasant disarray—the kind that you wanted to join and get in trouble with.

"You know, I still owe you," he said.

"This morning probably makes us even."

"I don't know. I did eat two of your sandwiches."

What was that Greek myth, about Hades and Persephone and pomegranates? Was this like that, where the peanut butter was the fruit, me the king of hell, and him a gender flipped personification of the spring?

"That is a lot of sandwiches," I heard myself say, without thinking.

I could see him fighting not to smile, desperately trying to play it cool. "Yeah, you know. I mean, that's the kind of thing it could take days of intense physical labor to work off. Months, even."

"Mmm," I agreed. "What kind of labor?"

"I could explain," he said, taking a step toward me. His blood started coursing through him, hoping—preparing—for where this was sure to lead.

"I don't know about that," I said, resting a hand on the knot of my towel. All of me wanted to be hard, but it'd be too easy for him to see right now, so I fought it.

"Then maybe I could just show you?" he asked, grinning shamelessly.

I laughed. "All right. But—I have to tell you what I tell everyone."

"What's that?" His brows rose, worried I was going to disclose some STD.

"I don't get attached. Ever. No matter how good this is—and I have a feeling it's going to be spectacular—I promise you nothing will change. You won't be the magical prince who cures me of my tomcat ways. There is literally no way you can be. So if you're looking for something real, you should go back to your place already."

He looked taken aback, and frowned slightly. "Who said I wanted anything more than a good time?"

Oh, just everything about him, the way he'd been interested in me since that fateful laundry night, the way he'd taken care of me this morning, and the spent the day here in the hopes of giving me head. I swallowed dryly. I could send him away for his own good—he was younger than me, even though we appeared the same age. But he was also a grown man, fully capable of making his own decisions—and if you had to learn a painful lesson about truth and the nature of upfront honesty in relationships, wouldn't you rather learn from someone who was fantastic in bed?

"I can show you a good time, all right," I said, my voice low, giving him a knowing smile. "Sit back down on the couch, Zach."

He considered his options for an instant, running away to shield his heart versus letting me have my way with him—and he retreated to the couch as if pulled there by a magnet.

"Good boy," I said, walking up. I hadn't dried myself off after my shower, I'd just wanted to deal with this situation—and now here I was, standing in front of him half-wet, water dripping from my hair down my chest toward the V of my hips, hidden by my orange towel.

He looked up at me, eyes full of expectation, wondering where this would lead, what I'd let him do. And I was cruel, I didn't give him any cues, I only waited for him to act.

Hesitantly, he reached his hands up and placed them on my stomach, feeling my skin at long last. He rocked forward and stroked them up the lean muscle of my abs and chest, kneading me with a slightly dropped jaw.

After that, there was no use in pretending. The hunger roared through me, searching for release, and I felt my cock grow hard. He was so close to it, stretched out catlike against me—and at seeing my towel rise one of his hands fell to its knot.

"Do it," I whispered, as he unwound the folds and it fell to the ground. One of his hands reached to hold me, as the other went and started at the buttons on his shirt, and he looked up.

"Are you clean?"

Of everything but vampirism. "Probably—but yeah," I had condoms in my bedroom—but in an instant I was released and he was fumbling behind him for his wallet. He pulled out a condom and pushed it on, following it immediately with his mouth, his green eyes staring up at me for approval. It was impossible not to give—I ran a hand through his hair and leaned forward with a groan.

His mouth started working my cock over, holding the condom down with one hand wrapped around my base as he rocked back and forth, letting the pressure of his tongue and lips roll back and forth against my shaft, sucking on my head. Every time he went in, he took me deep, I could feel my cock bending down his throat, and every time he pulled back he pressed his tongue against the sensitive skin of my tip.

It was a technique clearly honed with time—and on another person, probably somewhere in Florida. Their loss was my gain—I curled my hand into his hair and pulled him closer, I had a feeling he wanted to gag on me and—his throat closed as his eyes did, and I watched his blood sink down. I rocked his head on and off of me, feeling his throat grab against my head, as his saliva rained down on my balls.

I physically pulled him off my cock after that, holding him at arm's length by his hair, while he panted. He had a submissive streak and I'd tapped into it, he had that helplessly lost look of nearing subspace.

"Stay with me, cowboy." I demanded, tilting his head up to see me. "How many guys have you fucked, Zach?"

"Four?" he answered, like he was unsure.

"And how many guys have fucked you?"

"Ten," he said, much more confident.

"Good. Take off your clothing." I released him and stepped back to give him room to do so.

He stood up, a little shaky, reaching for the button he'd stopped at earlier. He unbuttoned the rest, tossed it aside, and then peeled his undershirt off. I'd been right. He hadn't been in Vegas long enough to lose his tan. I wanted to lick all his warm skin, and inside my mouth my fangs throbbed.

Zach missed all that, hurrying to unfasten his belt and push his slacks and boxers down. He stood up in just his socks shortly, as if presenting himself to me. He had a light tan line where his swim trunks had lived, and his cock was just as I remembered it, straight and firm.

"What do you want me to do next?" he inquired earnestly.

"Turn around."

He did as he was told, facing the couch. I brought my hands up to his shoulders, kneading them, bringing my body behind his, unafraid to touch skin to skin, letting him feel my hard on nudging at his waist. He smelled good—I kissed his neck where his shoulder met it—and he tasted even better.

I had my fill of the light in him, breathing him, touching him, tasting, rubbing my face against him like a cat, as my hands moved where they wanted. He stood still under this onslaught of attention, and then his hands reached back to touch pieces of me. I swatted them away, reaching forward around his waist to where his cock waited—and his hands reached back again.

"I meant it," I said, catching both of his wrists and yanking down. He melted a little under my presumed anger—I heard his breath catch, and so I didn't let him go. I nuzzled the nape of his neck, and his shoulder, as I brought his hands up behind him. "I get the feeling you don't always like being in control, Zach."

He swallowed audibly and then shook his head. "I don't."

"Good. Stay right there," I said, and then leaned down to pick up my towel. It was nothing to tear off a strip of it, and then use it to tie his arms together behind himself, each of his hands holding the opposite elbow. Turning him helpless in front of me, I held his arms back with one hand, as I reached around him to stroke his cock; rocking my hand back and forth, swirling his precum against his tip with my thumb as he moaned.

"Did I say you could moan?" I said. He quieted, and I laughed. "I'm kidding. I'm not a heartless bastard. Just a bastard is all," I went on, emphasizing my statements with my strokes. He made a guttural sound, but didn't open his mouth. "I want to use you in so many ways," I said, and returned one of my hands to my still condomed cock, to stroke it against him. "Bend over for me."

I held tight to the towel I'd wrapped his arms in as he did so, teetering precariously over my couch, reliant on my hold to balance him. I stroked my free hand down his back, to his ass, and spit where I meant to take him, and he shuddered in delight as I lined my cock up and slowly pushed in.

It didn't matter how many men someone'd been with—your first time with someone else, it was always polite to knock on the door before barging in. I controlled myself same as I controlled him, pushing him forward even as he wanted to sag back.

"Patience," I said, feeling him envelop me, piece by piece. His hips jerked and spasmed, trying to thrust if I wasn't going to, begging for friction. "Yeah?" I asked, rocking his body back and forth on me, as he bent lower to give me more of himself, trusting me not to drop him.

"Yeah," he breathed, as I closed the distance between us and settled deep.

We found a rhythm—or rather, I did, using his arms like a handle, bringing him onto me again and again as I leaned back and gloried in the sensation. Everything about him felt good to me, his mouth, his skin, his ass—I used a free hand to grab one glorious ass cheek and pull it wide so I could see the hot place where we met and—

"Can you," he began, his voice timid, "spank me?"

The thought made me harder. I was a creature of violent desires, who had very little chance to use them normally. I released his ass cheek, brought my arm back and swung down—stopping a centimeter over his soft skin. "Are you sure?"

"Yes. Please," he begged.

I brushed my hand over the place I was going to aim for, raised it up, and then smacked it down. It was halfway between a slap and a spank and he rose up on his toes before sinking back on me, harder.

"Again?" I asked, and he nodded. This time I used the other hand, with a little more force, and watched his supple flesh ripple. Fangs budded, unbidden. "What's your safeword, Zach?" I breathed.

"Dangerous," he said.

"Use it if you need to," I commanded—and I kept going.

I knew the terrible things I was capable of and so I didn't completely untether my hunger. But I let it come out to play, to feel the way he moved after I smacked him, listening to the way he gasped in pain and then grunted when my cock pounded back into him and it felt good, loving the way my handprints started to leave marks—it was all making me so hard, each time I pulled out I couldn't wait to get back into him—and then my fangs descended.

I stopped, mid-swing, pulling him back to me, willing my fangs back up into my palate.

"What happened?" he asked, oblivious to my struggle.

"Nothing," I said, lowering my hand. He moved provocatively, on purpose.

"I know you want it," he said.

"I do," I said, backing up. "But I'm a man in control of what he wants." I took a step back, and then another, until I was all the way out, and standing behind him. My hands went for the towel and untied him quickly.

He stumbled forward without meaning to, catching himself on the couch. "What's wrong?" he asked, looking back at me.

"That shit makes me hard as hell, but I want to see you when I come." I knew it was true the second I'd said it. The hunger didn't care who it fucked—but I did. "Come here." I sat down on the couch and grabbed him as I lay down, pulling him to straddle me with a minimum of fuss. "You don't mind, do you?" I asked as I reached between his legs to line my cock up with him again.

"Not at all."

"Then sit down." I arced my hips up and aimed my cock just right to fill his ass again. We both paused at the top of the arc to feel the sensations, me filling, him being full. "That's good," I whispered.

"Yeah," he said with a groan.

I moved subtly, feeling him in this new way, as he moved his own hips up and down. I had a much better view of him here, his lean body over mine, his hands on my shoulders as he both braced himself and rocked, and between us both, his balls and warm and heavy cock. I reached for it without thinking, and felt him stiffen as I took it in hand. His jaw dropped as I thrust up high with my hips— and started to stroke him.

"That's not fair," he protested.

"What's not?" I ran my hand up and down his shaft, starting to fuck his ass faster. He reacted by spreading his thighs wider apart to let me take him.

"You—you've got me—coming and going," he panted, in between my thrusts. The way he was moving over me, I could feel his ass squeezing as he made my cock line up inside himself to hit his spot.

"And what's wrong with that?" I asked, turned on by the way I was turning him on, stroking his cock. I let my other hand take over, and then spit into my first and returned it, lubricated.

He made a whining sound, as if it was causing him pain to hold out on me—and now my hips were bucking him high and his hands were curled into my shoulders and his cock was hard as I stroked it faster.

"I'm going to make you cum all over me, sunshine," I warned him —just before he did. He shouted, incoherent, and then his body thrashed, his ass grabbing onto my cock as silky white cum pumped out of him, spattering against my chest. And just like I'd thought, tasting his life was like biting into a perfect orange slice, cold, tangy, and sweet.

"Oh my God," he breathed, the first second he could do so, sagging over to lean against the couch. I panted beneath him, still sopping his orgasm up. "You're hard," he said in dismay.

I blinked back to life. "It's all right."

"No. I can't owe you again. I don't even know your name."

I reached a lazy hand over to press to his cheek. "It's Jack. And it's—"

The doorbell rang, cutting off whatever else I was going to say.

BOTH ZACH and I were still, like if we didn't move whomever was outside my apartment would go away—but they rang twice again in quick succession. And after everything that'd happened last night—I tapped Zach's ass to get him to get up and off of me and stood, picking up my towel to wrap around my waist again, now missing the bottom few inches, as I walked to look through my peephole.

Angela and Paco. *Shit.*

"Jack?" Angela asked, with a quaver.

"Coming!" I shouted, as Zach ran around my living room floor, trying to find his uniform, while I pulled the jeans I'd had on yesterday back on.

I heard Paco step forward and hit the doorbell again, just to bother me.

"Jesus," I said, opening up the door. Never had two more disparate groups of people met—I stood shirtless in the doorway, hopefully blocking the view of the young blonde man assembling himself behind me, while Angela's face was puffy from crying and her eyes were red, and Paco—Paco took things in and just glowered. *Shit. Shit. Shit.*

"Hey—are you all right?" I asked Angela. *Of course she wasn't—*

I saw her eyes flicker behind me and surely she could smell the sex wafting out—Paco too. "I just wanted to say thank you," she said, returning her attention to me, both her tone and expression flat. "You saved Rabbit's life last night, at great risk to your own, and I appreciate that."

"You're welcome."

"And—Dark Ink is closed for now, okay? Until further notice. I won't take it personally if you find another job."

"What?" I stepped forward, mostly closing the door behind me.

"It's just not safe there anymore."

I knew just enough about the Pack to press her—but it wasn't like she'd confess to being a werewolf in front of Paco—and I couldn't come clean about being a vampire with Zachary around, he'd already seen too much.

"Is there some time we can talk? Alone?" I asked.

She shook her head lightly. "You're not going to be able to change my mind, Jack."

"It's not like that. I just want to talk to you. Later tonight, if at all possible." I had an inkling of a plan—if she'd admit to me who she was, I might be able to help her.

"Tonight?" Everything about her seemed distracted.

"Please. I wouldn't ask if it weren't important."

She put a hand to her stomach like it hurt her. "Sure, yeah. Mark's place?"

"Yeah."

"I'll text you where," Paco said, gently taking her shoulders and steering her away. He cast a meaningful look over his shoulder at me, and I knew I had a lot to answer for.

CHAPTER TWENTY-TWO
JACK

I stepped back into my own apartment, where Zach had mostly assembled himself. "Who were they?" he asked.

"Friends."

"Both of them?"

"Yeah."

"He looks dangerous." The irony of him using his safeword to describe Paco did not elude me. "You two have history?"

"Yep." I reached for the waist of my jeans. I needed to shower again before I left home. "You'll find I have a history with a lot of guys. Which is why you should forget me."

"You're kidding me—I'm not going to leave you alone until I make you come."

"I guess that means you'll just have to keep trying," I said without thinking as I unzipped my fly. He looked momentarily hopeful. "But not right now."

"No." His shoulders slumped. "I've got to get to work."

"I hope you have another uniform. And time for a shower."

"I do, and barely."

"Good." We stood, facing each other like duelists in the old west, his hands in his pockets and my hands on my waistband. "Get going, Zach," I said, lightly shaking my head.

He swept his shirt up off the ground. "See you—Jack." He said my name separately, like it was a codeword—and then went for the door. I locked it behind him and sat down with my phone and pulled up Paco's name and sent him three texts.

Address?

What kind of clients does your boss represent?

And—I can explain.

I tossed my phone onto my bed, and hopped back into the shower.

BY THE TIME I came out of shower number two he'd responded with Mark's address—Mark lived on Eagles Landing Lane, south of Vegas, in hills with a distant view of the Strip—*casino interests*, and *don't bother*.

That's what I'd been hoping about Mark's clientele. You didn't make a lot of money working the DUI/worker's comp circuit in this city—to afford Paco and his ilk, he had to be making big bucks, which meant he had big connections, which was good because there was no way I was going to sell my idea to Rosalie otherwise.

I'd realized halfway through my fight with Daziel that I couldn't take on an entire gang of werewolves alone—and killing them off individually would take too long, and leave Angela far too exposed. Which meant that I—and Paco, and whomever else Mark had hired —needed back-up: which meant asking Rosalie.

She'd have a price, of course, and it might be too high to afford, but I wouldn't know until I'd asked her.

I pulled on clean jeans, a nice shirt, and my new leather jacket courtesy of Francesca, and killed a few hours, before hailing an Uber back to my car at Angela's apartment complex.

FORTY-FIVE MINUTES AFTER THAT, I was parked outside Vermillion, again. I'd spent the past ten minutes just sitting there, perfecting a pitch in my head and planning how I was going to get in and out without getting roped into doing sexual favors for half the club's clientele.

After that, I steeled myself, got out of the car, and marched in. The girls inside flocked around me until they recognized me, and then blew me off, as I walked to the bar. The night was young, and there were only a few men here, most of them were at tables or waiting by the main stage, and I took my spot in the queue.

"He's in back," said the man next to me, companionably.

"He?" I asked, as the back door swung open. And just like in my very infrequent but always traumatizing nightmares, Tamo emerged —only this time he was holding trays of clean glassware.

I should've run but I froze instead, refusing to believe that it was him. Then he set the glassware down and looked over, the scar I'd given him on his forehead clearly visible.

"Jack. Long time no see."

"Yeah." Did he remember how I killed him? I'd been so careful....

Rosalie came out of the same door. "My two favorite boys!" she said, and clapped her hands, then scanned the room past us until she saw who she liked, gesturing at a girl, and then pointing at the bar. An unnamed stripper walked forward to man it, as Rosalie went to the side, and looked to me. "Come on back, Jack."

And like the dutiful vampire she compelled me to be, I followed.

THE THREE OF us were in the small kitchen behind Vermillion's bar, with Tamo taking up most of the space. Death hadn't made him any thinner.

"I thought you were...." I began slowly.

"Dead? Only for a little while." He turned and smiled at Rosalie.

"Like a little while at the time? Or like she went and dug you up?"

"Don't be gauche, Jack. I knew you two didn't get along, and I didn't want either of you to come up with ideas, so I've been very carefully keeping you apart."

"Until tonight."

"I didn't expect you to visit twice in a row—and I was afraid you'd drop werewolves on my club. If a werewolf showed up here, you couldn't blame me for wanting Tamo at my side." She was sidled up against him, like a cat, and he wrapped a possessive arm around her—and now I realized why she used me infrequently and had the patience to deal with my refusals—because Tamo was not the refusing type. "So why are you here again?"

I looked from one to the other of them. "Because of the weres—and because of a possible business opportunity."

Rosalie tilted her head. "I'm listening."

"Say the woman I'm protecting had the backing of a major casino —what would it take for you to fight by her side?"

Tamo named an absurd amount of money, and Rosalie shook her head. "No—that's short-sighted. Why would you take a flat fee, when you can install a printing press?"

"I don't follow," I said.

"A club of my own on the strip, as part of their casino. They'd give us space, we'd leverage their discounts on liquor, and we'd have more of a dance floor for the proles, but we'd keep my extraordinary girls in back to dance, at triple the rates they ask for here."

"Sounds like you've thought about this before," Tamo said.

"Because I have," Rosalie agreed, then returned her attention to me. "But there's only three, maybe four, hotels there that have both the money and the space."

"What form of protection would you be offering in exchange?"

Her eyes narrowed. "Depends on the contract, and the club. Anything from night-time guards to a private desert bunker."

I was surprised to hear about that, but Tamo wasn't. A bunker sounded much more guardable than a house—especially when the vampire guards would be asleep during the day. "How could I guarantee the bunker option?"

"A club at the Fleur De Lis, of course," she answered without thinking. "I don't have a French accent for nothing, Jack."

Only the newest and most expensive hotel on the Strip. I rocked back on my heels. "I'll see what I can do."

"Good. But don't dare dream of involving us until contracts are signed, which, quite frankly, I don't see happening. And don't you dare expose our kind to them to get them to sign. None of them must know. Mortals that know begin to get ideas, and I find ideas intolerable."

I nodded. Her terms were understandable, and I could hardly expect vampires to expose themselves otherwise.

Her expression changed from cruel to cat-like. "So would you like to stick around? I'm sure I can find agreeable work for you to do." Her lips lifted in a tease.

"No, I'm fine tonight, thank you," I said quickly, backing out of the kitchen and into the bar.

I WENT STRAIGHT from the bar out into the parking lot, and was halfway to my car when, *"Jack, wait,"* compelled me.

I stood stock still, facing forward, hearing the sound of Rosalie's heels walk up behind. She rounded me and looked obstinately up. "Did you honestly think I didn't know what happened?"

And this was why she'd never compelled me to tell her the truth—she already knew it. "I thought he was dead," I said, trying to play it off. I'd overdosed him on sleeping pills and insulin—one to knock him out, the other to put him into a coma that he'd die from.

"Well I'm sure the dawn was coming, and you couldn't stick around long enough to find out."

"But his heart...."

She slapped me, hard. "What do you know of his heart?"

The fierce way she was looking at me now—and the way she'd been with him in the kitchen—my mistress was in love. It was a strange look for her. "He wanted to kill me," I said, as my hand cradled my cheek—if I were a mere mortal, she would've broken my jaw.

"And I should've let him, seeing how poorly you've repaid me for the gifts I've bestowed on you." Rosalie folded her hands in and looked unflappable again. "I've known what you've done this whole time, and never told you. Think on that. Think on all the things that I probably know, and as of yet have no cause to share."

Paco, Angela—hell, now, even Zach. I grit my teeth and looked down.

"As it was, you merely forced my hand. My sweet Tamo knows nothing, content to enjoy his every day here in the forever-life with me. And while I don't think he'd regret being turned—I've never seen a man take so well to it—he might have cause to be angry about the manner of his turning. Especially since there was no way you could know *I* was to save him, and *you* wanted him to die the final death."

"I had to protect myself," I muttered. She snorted to let me know what she thought of that.

"Come back with a contract in hand, and then we'll see about helping. Until then, if you die, die alone like a dog," she said, dismissing me with one hand as she turned to go back to her club. I watched her go and waited until the door had shut behind her to get into my car.

CHAPTER TWENTY-THREE
ANGELA

I f there was one thing Paco and I could agree on, it was silence. He drove the car, looking at all the mirrors frequently, to make sure we weren't being followed, and to check on me in the back seat. I was tangled in a ball, my knees up under my chin, my skirt wrapped around them, my sandals on the nice leather interior without thinking, hugging one hand around my midriff, the other playing mindlessly with the zippers on the duffle.

My stomach hurt. I'd never taken so much silver before at once— but *she'd* never been so close to coming out of me, either. I was worried about her—and worried about me. Would she come back? Had I poisoned her—and in doing so, poisoned myself? I didn't know. And it was hard to muster the strength to care because of my mom.

What the fuck had Gray been thinking? Was killing my mother intentional? Meant to send a message to me about how far they'd go? Or was she just a tragic accident, just another casualty in our family-sized war?

The bloody rabbit...now that was a message. They wanted him, and they were tired of waiting for me. Either behave—or it'll be your blood up on the wall, and you'll still lose him.

It was time for us to do the only thing we could—the thing we should've done months, no years, ago—run.

And I wouldn't go back for my tattoo guns, this time.

THE CAR PULLED us into the circular driveway at Mark's, past two armed guards at the door. Mark's home was an eight bedroom palace almost half-an-hour out of town built to highlight dramatic views through bulletproof glass.

The men nodded to me as I got out of the car and went in.

Vaulted ceilings, amazing staircases—my mother's death had solved the problem of how Mark would manage to make a scooter-mover look tasteful, at least. I ran a hand through my hair, cursing my dark sense of humor, and struggling not to cry. This was the kind of life my mother had dreamed of for me and now—

"Momma?" Rabbit's voice echoed from somewhere up above. "Momma!"

I raced toward him, instinctively.

He was three rooms in on the second floor, in a guest bedroom done up in swags of deep maroon and army green. I burst in on him, finding him tangled in his sheets, in the throes of a nightmare. "Momma!" he shouted out.

I sank onto the bed beside him. "Shh. It's okay, I'm here now, shh."

He struggled a little, made a puppy-whine, and then relented.

How long had it been since I'd given him silver? Who would know to give him silver if anything happened to me? I smoothed his brow with one hand, and reached into my bag with the other. Just sticking my finger into the colloidal silver bottle burned—but my fingertip retrieved a drop, and with my other hand, I opened up his mouth a little and let it fall—burning him same as it'd burned me.

"This is all my fault," I said, kissing him on his cheeks and fore-head. "I'm so sorry, baby."

"You're wrong," said a voice from the doorway. I turned and saw Mark, standing there with crossed arms.

"What?"

"It's not your fault. It only feels that way right now." He put his hand out for me, and I ignored it, choosing instead to straighten Rabbit's covers, pulling him a toy out of the duffle bag to snuggle near. Then and only then, I stood—and carefully walked through the doorway without touching him. There were three cars in the drive-way, surely Mark didn't carry around three sets of keys—or maybe I should get a rental—*no*—I'd take one of Mark's cars, drive to Barstow, and then get a rental—distance first, distance was imperative—

"Angela, please don't shut me out."

"It's your house, I could hardly manage to." The last time I'd seen car keys here they'd been on his desk—I started walking fiercely down the hall, with him close behind. I turned and went into his office—it was twice the size of his one at work, in almost every respect—bigger desk, bigger couch, even more certificates on the wall proclaiming he was a respectable citizen.

"I know you're hurting Angie, but please," he said, more firmly blocking the door, as I went through the papers on his desk, searching for keys I couldn't find.

I whirled on him. "I know you love me—but I don't love you."

He looked gravely wounded at that. "Angela," he groaned.

"I was only fucking you so that you would kill Gray."

"That's a lie and you know it."

I reached the last stack on his desk and swiped it off, papers flut-tering to the ground. "If he were dead already, this wouldn't be happening, but he's not, because you can't, because no one can—and now Rabbit and I need to get the fuck away. Give me keys!"

Mark took one step in and then another, hands held high. "You're acting crazy Angie—stop that."

"You're the crazy one! Thinking you can love me!" I shoved a paperweight off his desk and it dropped putting a solid ding in the undoubtedly expensive reclaimed barnwood floor. "You don't even *know* me!"

"Yes, I do."

"No! You don't!" I shouted at him, at full force. I was tired of pretending—I was tired of everything—I grabbed the top of my shirt with both my hands and ripped it open. "See?" I said, dropping every wall I had, waiting for *her* to race out and frighten him. Only *she* wasn't there right now, after all the silver I'd chugged to send her away.

I couldn't even get that right. I fell to my knees, sobbing.

Mark squatted on his heels not that far away. "Angela," he said, much more kindly than I deserved. "You've had a long day and a shittier night. Let's pretend this didn't happen, all right?"

"I'm a werewolf, Mark. And so is Gray. And if you don't let me leave right now with Rabbit, he's going to come and kill you."

Mark gave me a pitying look, and scooped me up. "Come on. I've got some sleeping pills in my bedroom."

I LET Mark put me on his bed, undress me, and then put me underneath the sheets, all with infinite care. "You're tiny, so," he explained as he snapped a pill in half, before sticking it in my mouth. I only had a moment to taste the bitterness, before he offered me a swig of water and relief.

I doubted twelve of anything could put me under right now—but within minutes I felt the urge to sleep come on me like a wave and take me out.

I woke three hours later, because the clock on the nightstand said it was only midnight. I stirred, feeling Mark's high thread count sheets hold me, and then I heard him.

"You were supposed to sleep longer," he said, looking down

and over. He was mostly clothed—his shoes and suit jacket were off, and he was propped up against a pile of pillows, reading a tablet. He had reading glasses on, ones I'd never seen him wear before.

"Was I?"

"Only because you needed it." He reached over and pressed a hand to my forehead like a concerned mom. "You've had a long day."

The safe envelope of sleep burst, and everything that'd happened —my mother, the blood, our fight—settled back down, pressing the life from me. "Yeah," I agreed, softly.

His thumb stroked the furrows of my brow. "Are you feeling any better?"

I shook my head no.

"You said some crazy things. Still think you're a werewolf?"

I searched inside myself. *She* was nowhere to be found. "No." Me getting committed to an insane asylum would make it a hundred times easier for the Pack to steal Rabbit.

"K." He returned his hand to his tablet and used it to stroke a page aside.

"What're you reading?"

"Complicated women and how to love them," he said dryly. I snorted. "It's a New Yorker."

"Of course it is," I said, and rolled over, showing him my back.

"What's that supposed to mean?"

"That we're from different worlds. Even if you work with mobsters now—you work with high class mobsters. It's different."

There was utter and extreme silence from his half of the bed. I knew he was getting ready to lawyerize at me. "I'm sick to death of this 'I don't deserve you bullshit,' Angela. You're the only one who thinks you're stuck in a fairytale."

"If I were stuck in a fairytale, my mom wouldn't have died."

That shut him up. "I'm sorry."

"Me too." I curled into a ball.

I heard him set the tablet down and felt the bed move as he came to lay beside me, wrapping himself around me on top of the covers like a big spoon. "You should go back to sleep."

"Why? It doesn't fix anything."

"It might help, if you let it." His free hand brushed through my hair. "I'll be here, watching over you all night."

"Gray is going to come after me and Rabbit."

He worried his chin against the back of my head. "There's ten guys out there, in between us and him.

"That's not enough."

"How many will it take to make you feel safe? Twenty? Thirty? A hundred?" He wrapped his arm around me and held me tight. "Only if they have silver knives?" he teased.

"It's not me. It's you. I can't have anything happen to you, too." I put a sheet-wrapped knuckle into my mouth at the thought of losing him.

"And you said you didn't love me." I could hear his tone—droll, but hopeful.

"I lied," I confessed.

I heard him swallow softly. "I know these are shitty circumstances...but can I hear you say it?"

I twisted my head up to look at him, largely shadowed by his jaw. "I love you, Mark. I probably have for a while now, I just didn't want to...." My voice faded as I lost strength.

"To what?" he asked.

"Let you know. Not because I was worried about giving away the upper hand or any rom-com stuff—but because of stuff like this. And because I wanted you to say it first."

He bent his head and took my chin and made our lips align. "I love you, Angela," he breathed into me, looking down, and kissed me gently.

My body instantly warmed. Everything that'd happened—just like sleep could make you forget for a moment, sex could too, if you let it, if you did it right. I spun in the sheets to face him, and as he leaned in, I started pushing them down.

CHAPTER TWENTY-THREE

He intuited my purpose quickly. "You're sure?" he breathed.

"Yes. Please. I love you," I said, and started working at the buttons at his throat. He leaned back and went for his waistband, pushing his boxers and slacks clear but not all the way off—then he grabbed my wrists and pushed me back, laying on top of me, still with half his clothes on.

"Say it again."

"I love you," I whispered. I could feel him hard against me, and I tilted my hips up to catch him.

He kissed me deeply, then, "Again."

"I love you," I whispered breathlessly, as he reached down to push my underwear aside and then push in.

I put one leg over him and gave myself over to the moment, as his kisses ravished my mouth and neck, as we rocked. All the movements were small, but amplified by the care both of us took with each other. We were now two people in love, and both of us knew it. He let go of my wrists and I found his hair with one hand and went down his back with the other to pull up his shirt. Still kissing me, we turned, so that I was on top, riding and rubbing myself against him.

"God, I love you, Angela," he repeated, looking up at me, reaching up to hold my hair back so that he could see more of me as I straddled him. I wanted to touch more of his still clothed skin, but I knew there wasn't time—the release of emotions made it so intense—I grabbed hold of his shirt and clawed it into my hands.

"Mark," I warned him.

"Keep going," he growled. "I want to see the woman I love come."

I held onto his shirt to keep me upright and then rode his cock, hard and fast, rubbing myself more into him each time, feeling the need for release scrape up from deep inside, ready to wring me out, as I used my lover's cock to screw me to oblivion—

"Oh my God—Mark!" I shouted, helplessly, as the first wave hit me and took me down. I fell forward with the force of it, but that didn't stop the next wave from slamming close behind. "Mark—Mark—Mark," I said and kept rocking my hips against him.

"Yes," he purred beneath me, feeling my pussy squeeze him tight. I wound up flat and panting on his chest like a shipwreck survivor who'd just found land—then his hands reached for my waist, and I looked up.

"Oh fuck me Mark, please," I breathed—because I knew he wanted to hear it, and because the longer we were here the longer I could keep reality at bay.

He braced his feet on his bed and had his way with me, holding my hips down while he pounded up or making me fuck him in turn. My breasts were going to have rug burn from his shirt, and a line of bruises from his buttons, but I didn't mind—I needed to be wanted, brutally, just like this. I reached back to spread myself wider, to take more of him in—I arched my hips up, to give all of myself to him, and he moaned at getting such perfect and eager submission. It made him harder, knowing that I was ceding myself and—his hands holding my ass clenched as I heard him gasp and then his hips thrust into me fully, another perfect ten times and—he groaned deeply, wildly, as I felt his entire cock twitch and bob inside me, his load surely shooting out.

"Angela," he breathed, when next he could. I lay atop him, dizzy. If I truly loved him, I had to leave—but if I truly loved him, I couldn't break his heart like that, not even for his own good. No, the second *she* came back I would—

"Angela," he murmured, moving to cradle me, holding me in his arms against his chest. "I love you so much."

I moved to softly kiss his jaw. "I love you too," I whispered.

Even if it's going to be the death of us.

CHAPTER TWENTY-FOUR
JACK

I pulled my car into Mark's driveway at a quarter to one—or rather, I would have, if several well-suited men with radios in one hand and the other reaching for holstered guns hadn't blocked me. Then they got some sort of answer they agreed with from their radios and waved me through, one of them watching me, one of them back to staring out at the beyond. I wheeled in slowly, and put my car into park, just as Paco came out.

"You're early," he said, expression unreadable.

"Usually being punctual is a good thing, right?"

"Not in this case," he said, turning around for me to follow him in.

I always sort of knew that Mark had style. Being wealthy was no guarantee of it, I'd seen enough rich people make fools of themselves on the Strip over the years. But his house—his mansion—was tastefully appointed, the furniture welcoming but spare, the colors saturated but almost monochromatic.

"Done gawking?" Paco asked, leading me into a drawing room, complete with a billiard table, wet bar, and a fireplace. I bet this house had all the rooms on the Clue board.

"Almost," I said, turning to smile at him. He did not smile in return. "Look, Paco...."

"I said don't bother explaining in my text, didn't I?"

"And since when do I ever listen to your good advice?" I walked around to be standing in front of him.

His eyes narrowed. "Not often enough."

He seemed angry—he was always kind of angry, it went with his past and his profession, but this was beyond that. This time he was angry at me. "What's this about, Paco?"

He stepped near and leaned in. "I never even get to visit your apartment, and then today I find you fucking some stranger on your couch?"

I sank back. "The cops kept me last night for as long as they could—the kid's a neighbor, he caught me coming in this morning at sunrise. If he hadn't dragged me into my apartment, you and Angela would've been visiting a pile of ashes in the parking lot."

Paco's anger shifted only slightly toward concern. "So he knows?"

"No. I kept it together until I got inside, and he's not the nosy type."

"But he *is* your type, though."

"Everyone's my type," I said, flippantly.

"Apparently," Paco said, just as flippant back.

That's what it was. He was jealous of Zachary. "Paco," I said, my voice going low.

He shrugged one shoulder, blowing me off. "I always knew it'd be a matter of time."

"Until what?"

"Until you replaced me. One way or another."

"Do you really think I'm like that?" I tilted my head at him. "I mean I know our shit is complicated, but is that who you think I am?"

"Jack, look at me. We started off the same age. But now I'm getting older than you...."

"I'm not ditching you for a younger model, trust me," I said.

"But it's never going to be like it was," he went on. "I can't go back."

"And I don't want to! I don't want what we had—I want what we have."

His dark eyes pierced me. "Just what is that, Jack? And in ten or twenty or forty years, what's that going to be?"

I stared at him, the singular point of safety and sanity I'd had ever since I'd been turned. "I'm sorry that we can't be normal, Paco. I wish to Christ we could. But I swear, whenever you wind up in a nursing home someday, all the attendants will think you have the most handsome great-grandson ever, and that when the door is closed if I can't fuck you or suck you or jerk you off anymore, then I will climb in to your bed and just hold you tight till morning."

He was silent for a long time. "Fuck you, Jack."

"I mean it, Paco."

He swallowed. "I do too. Fuck you. For being a vampire."

Instead of being a real man. "I know. But if I wasn't, I never would've met you."

A moment passed between us, the acknowledgement of the things we had, and things we'd never be, then Paco broke it with a sigh. "Your boss and my boss are upstairs again."

"Again? For how long?"

"You tell me." He walked over to the fireplace and put his hands out.

"How many cameras are in this room?"

His eyes flicked over, and he gestured to two corners, where they covered the door. But there was a hidden alcove by the pool cue display. I walked into it. "C'mere."

He looked back at me and shook his head.

"I don't think you heard me. *Come. Here,*" I said, and his feet walked him over.

"That's not fair," he complained. But we'd played these games before, and I knew he wasn't frightened of me—especially when he reached up to take his ear piece out.

"Neither is this," I said, falling to my knees, and reaching for his belt buckle.

"I'm on duty, Jack."

"And I have ears like a bat. Like literally, like a bat," I said, pushing his slacks and boxers down and pulling his cock out. I went for it, instantly, wrapping my lips around it, savoring the feeling of him growing hard as my mouth held him.

He wound his hand in my hair and pushed me back. "My professional reputation is on the line."

"So's mine," I said, and went back in.

He fought for one second longer, and then fell back against the wall behind him to brace, jutting his hips out for me. I held his shaft with one hand, his balls with the other, and then kissed the head of him like I might never get the chance to again, voraciously, running my tongue and lips around all of his soft edges, trying to make him feel what I did, that there was a reason we'd found each other—that we were meant to be. I heard his breath speed up above, and his hand in my hair clawed in passion, as I alternated between taking him deep inside my throat, pressing myself against his belly, almost making myself gag, to pulling almost all the way off of him with my mouth while stroking with my hand, so that no part of him was ever left uncovered or untouched.

He groaned low. We'd done this a hundred—maybe a thousand times— and I'd never get tired of hearing that sound. I moaned my pleasure back at him and started, with my mouth and with my hands, begging for him to come.

Slowly Paco's other hand crept forward to also hold my head, and then he took control, pulling me on and off of him, burying himself up to his hilt only rock me back and expose his shining shaft as he fucked my face, giving me all of him only to take it back, leaving me panting and wanting more—if this was penance for scaring him, I would gladly pay, again and again and again—I brought my tongue up to stroke the bottom of his cock, wrapped my lips so that each stroke was tight, closed my throat so that it grabbed him every time he bobbed. I knew him so well—I knew exactly when—

His fingers grabbed hold of my hair and he shoved forward fast and hard, sealing my mouth around his base as his hard hot cock bent down my throat inside me, and I looked up, watching him lose himself as I felt his body jerk and spasm as his cum poured out. He was gasping quietly, his hips thrusting as he held my mouth tight, giving his load to me, until he sagged against the wall and one of his hands let go. The life that Paco gave me was beautiful—it always would be. I rocked back slowly, relishing releasing him, the sensitive shudders that my tongue could still cause, as I carefully licked up every drop. And when his cock was flaccid in front of me, I kissed it gently then too, and set it back inside his shorts, helping him to pull his pants up. His eyes were glazed, his focus distant, but he reached out a hand for me to hold my jaw and trace my lips with his thumb.

"Better?" I asked him.

"A little," he answered, as I rocked up to standing.

"Good. 'Cause I'm gonna get a lot of play at that nursing home."

His hands paused on his belt buckle. "What?"

"I bet I could bleed a lot of people at a nursing home—everyone's always expecting them to die."

Paco closed his eyes and shook his head. "You're sick, Jack."

"And you love me because of it," I said, kissing him. I heard a muffled scream of pleasure upstairs, and I went for the wet bar, to swish and spit and wash my hands.

CHAPTER TWENTY-FIVE
ANGELA

Mark was still holding me when there was a knock at our door. I felt his arms tense, as if he might have to protect me personally. "What is it?" he barked.

"There's someone here to see you, Miss Wilshire."

"Who?" he asked.

Oh shit. I'd completely forgotten. "Jack," I answered, before security could.

"What?" Mark asked, twisting toward me. "Why?"

"He'd asked to talk to me alone." I started to move away from Mark, disentangling myself from the sheets. I'd left the duffle full of my clothes in Rabbit's room, of course—I'd have to sneak down there and get it, or just wear what I'd had on.

"That's not going to happen," Mark said, and I didn't know if he was talking to security or me.

"I told him I would."

"You're in grief right now. He's taking advantage of you."

"To be fair, I did just tell him today that Dark Ink was closed, and he should start looking for a new job." I guess it didn't matter if my clothes were dirty, all of me needed a shower after that fucking. And speaking of fucking—I knew exactly what Paco and I had interrupted at Jack's house earlier on. "Plus, he's gay."

Mark sat up on the edge of his bed. "Gay-gay, or gay like you are?"

I paused, bra halfway clasped. "Good question."

"Look, Angela, I get that you want to keep doing things so that you don't have to slow down and feel your feelings. I've had people die, I've been there myself. It may feel important at the time, but believe me, you're just postponing the inevitable."

I sighed. "Trust me, I already feel plenty bad. And I know about postponing things, all right?" I pulled my shirt back on over my head. "Postponing things is like my superpower."

"Hmm?"

"Never mind. Just—he saved Rabbit's life. Let me do this, and then it'll be done, okay? He drove all the way out here." I pulled my hair back into a knot, and went for the door.

PACO WAS WAITING POLITELY OUTSIDE, and he made no comment about my appearance as he wove us through Mark's mansion and down into the wine cellar.

"Here?" I hugged myself. It was cold—and maybe Mark was right to worry.

As if reading my mind Paco said, "I promise nothing bad will happen to you. I give you my word." His handsome face was solemn and he seemed sincere.

"Sure." Why not? What else could possibly happen to me today? He left the room, and I started reading dusty wine labels in French, one eye on the door.

And even then, I didn't see him. It was like one moment the room was empty, and the next he was there. "Hey, Ang." Jack had on a black leather jacket—it was a new one, I hadn't seen before—and jeans and a shirt and a troubled stare.

"Jack," I said with a tight smile. In normal times we might hug—but for whatever reason, this time did not feel normal. "Thanks again."

"I only wish I'd gotten there sooner."

"I'm not sure. I don't think you could've saved her and him." He'd gone up against a werewolf for me—without knowing. "You're lucky to be alive. Honestly."

"Yeah?" he asked and then paused, as if waiting for more.

"Yeah," I said, closing the book of his question. "What'd you want to see me alone for, Jack?"

It was a small room—but that didn't stop him from pacing. Then, deciding something, he stopped and looked at me. "I don't think we have much time, so I'm going to cut to the chase. What would happen to you if I touched you with silver?"

Oh God. He'd managed to injure a Pack member—I should've thought to wonder how, but I'd been so busy with Rabbit and with crying and with Mark. "What?" I laughed, trying to play the question off as silly. "Why would you ask?"

"Please. Cut the crap, Angela. I know. About you—and Rabbit. I know."

"Know what?"

Jack pulled a knife out of his pocket and set it down on the stone table in the center of the room. "Touch it then. Or, keep playing games."

And *that* was how. Who carries a silver knife with them, and why? But we'd worked together for years and he'd never suspected—or, had he? I didn't know.

"Just touch it, Angie," he said, grabbing my wrist to yank it forward—before letting me go and jumping back to look at his hand, mystified. "You—you stung me."

"What the fuck Jack, this isn't funny," I said, sidling toward the door, ready to run.

"Goddammit Angela," he said and grabbed my shoulders to hold me back, carefully only touching where my shirt was. "Just—look at me."

I scrunched up my eyes and inhaled to scream.

"Be quiet and look!" he hissed.

My scream withered and my eyes snapped open and—there was Jack, my employee, and friend, standing in front of me with fangs. And suddenly so many things made sense—the way I'd never gotten him to work a shift before sundown, the way he'd never come to any of Rabbit's birthday parties, how if you called him during the day he'd never, ever, answer.

His fangs retracted slowly. "You can talk now. Sorry. I just had to show you. And I can make you forget, if you want to."

"No," I answered quickly.

He nodded at that. "Okay."

I looked between him and the knife. "So...you know?"

"I guessed. Not until recently. And I still don't know why touching you burns me—it didn't that first time we met, back in the day."

I walked over to the table. "I take silver. So does Rabbit. It keeps the wolf down." That was the first time I'd as much as admitted it, to someone who might believe me.

"That explains it then," he said.

"Are there others?" I asked him.

"Like me and like you? Yes. And there's people that use magic. Past that, I'm not sure, but I don't take anything for granted anymore."

I nodded. The silver knife was mesmerizing—my hand darted out and touched its blade. It stung like a hot curling iron, and I bit my lips to stop from screaming. *"Shit."*

"Yeah. It burns me, too. Maybe not as bad though." He rounded the table to be across from me. "Angela, if the Pack is after you because of Rabbit—they're not going to let you go. And you're not safe here. You have to know that."

"I do. But I don't have anywhere else to go."

"I've been kind of working on that. I have a plan. But I need your help to pull it off."

"You? Have a plan?" I gawked at him. "I'm sorry, that sounded bad—I mean—it's the Pack. Who can stop them?"

"The person who made me can offer protection, for a price."

I shrank back, trying to figure out what I could sell Dark Ink for, and how fast I could be liquid. "How much?"

"More than you could ever hope to pay. But your boyfriend—would he really do anything for you?"

I nodded. Mark had put a hit on Gray for crying out loud. "Yeah."

"Who the hell does he work for?" Jack asked.

"I don't know who—but I know where." We'd been there often enough. "The Fleur De Lis."

Jack rocked back. "Fucking-a. If he's willing to deal with some business people I know, you can get guards—like me." He pointed to where his fangs had been. "Or a bunker to hole up in, somewhere even the Pack won't be able to find."

"Jack, they've scented me. They can follow me anywhere."

He looked worried for a moment, but then shook it off. "I refuse to believe that. Or if they can, I'm sure my boss can figure a way to set you free."

"Your boss?" I asked.

"My other boss." He gave me a sad half-smile. "I don't like her as much as I like you."

The words were...honest. And it was just the two of us in this tiny space—and I remembered the night we met, the way we'd been all over each other. Somewhere deep inside me my wolf swung her tail like a slow drum's beat.

She'd always known what Jack was—the biggest, baddest guy in the room.

Who would've guessed my knight in shining armor would have quite so many tattoos?

I heard a scuffle from outside, same as Jack did, but he turned to me more quickly. *"You are forbidden from telling anyone else of my kind,"* he said, and suddenly I felt compelled to silence, at least where vampires were concerned.

"Same, same," I said as Mark burst in, Paco close behind. "I'm firing you," he growled at Paco.

"Sir," Paco protested, as Mark took in the room, Jack's presence, and the silver knife.

"Mark, don't," I said.

"Somehow he takes you to the only room in the house where I can't see what's going on?" Mark pointed between the two other men like they were in cahoots.

"I was making the lady an offer," Jack said. Mark's eyes flashed—not threatened, just pissed.

"Which was?" he asked archly.

"As you suspected, Jack's involved in some stuff," I cut in, putting myself between them, resting my hands on Mark's broad chest. "He knows some people, who know some people, who have a bunker in the desert."

"For a price," Jack corrected.

"What a true friend," Mark sneered.

Jack shrugged, pretending that Mark wasn't getting to him, no matter how much I could feel the tension ratcheting. "It's not my bunker."

"She doesn't need a bunker—I have my house, and my men."

"One of whom you just fired," Jack said.

"Paco!" Mark shouted, apparently ready to rehire him now—if only to escort Jack off the premises. When Paco didn't readily respond, he shouted again, louder. "Paco!"

I'd only known the man for a few days, and I already knew disobedience wasn't like him—and I saw something akin to abject worry momentarily cross Jack's face—until Paco appeared on the stairs to the room.

"Sir!" Paco shouted back, with one hand on his ear piece.

"There's been a fight at the prison. Gray's been injured—they're moving him to the infirmary."

Was this it? I gasped and looked to Mark, watching his jaw clench. "That wasn't me," he said, all but admitting to everyone in this small room that that'd been his plan. "After your mother's murder, there would've been too much heat—I called it off."

"But, maybe?" I asked.

"No. I'm sorry, Ang. I meant to tell you—we'll have to figure out another way—or use the legal system, God help us."

"That's good though, right?" Jack said.

"Yeah, anyone who stabs that fucker deserves a medal in my book," Mark said.

They kept talking as my thoughts faded out, staring at the silver knife in front of me. Gray wasn't stupid, he'd always be using the minimum amount of silver he needed just to get by—to keep his wolf down around the full moon. While a full moon was coming up —there was no way just anyone had stabbed him. He must've wanted to be stabbed. But why?

"Are prison infirmaries as secure as the rest of the place?" I asked, interrupting Mark and Jack's continued conversation.

Paco's eyes met mine over their heads, from the stairs. "Notably less so."

"They're going to break him out of prison."

I'd said it mostly to myself, but both Jack and Mark's heads turned as what I'd said sunk in.

"Shit!" Mark cursed.

Jack instantly reached out his hand to Mark. "Whether you believe it or not, we both have Angela's best interests at heart. Let me put you in touch with my friends."

Mark hesitated.

"If I'm not still fired, I'd recommend that you listen to him," Paco said.

"Please, baby," I added.

Mark looked at me, and then shook Jack's hand. "All right."

Both of them stood there for a moment, sizing the other up just in case. The second their hands released, I took Mark's and turned to Jack. "How soon can we get there?"

THE STORY CONTINUES IN

Blood by Moonlight: Dark Ink Tattoo Book Four

READ ON FOR A SNEAK PEEK.

BLOOD BY MOONLIGHT
DARK INK TATTOO BOOK FOUR
JACK

"How soon can we get there?" Angela asked, wide-eyed, now that her man Mark and I had made our deal. And *there* was the werewolf-proof, vampire-guarded bunker in the desert my Mistress could provide for them, if they agreed to her terms.

Angela's question echoed in the small room, as I started thinking.

Rosalie would be thrilled to have Mark's money, of course, and the Fleur de Lis's backing—but—my eyes flickered over to Paco, who knew I was a vampire, and so was surely thinking the same thing: *how close was it to dawn?*

It was already late. What if Mark drove a hard bargain? Or worse yet—what if Rosalie whammied him into an easy one? Once he was in the door, who knew?

And then on top of that, what was the Pack's timeframe?

"Well?" Mark asked, looking at me.

"We're going to Vermillion," I said.

"The strip club downtown?" he asked.

"Yeah." I snatched my knife back off the table and pocketed it. "I'll meet you there—I need to pave the path with some introductions."

"But you made it sound like," Angela began, worry creeping back.

"It'll be fine. Bring Paco and then leave him in the car—the place itself is safe." I pushed past them for the stairs.

"I've met the owner of Vermillion socially—and I know Vegas," Mark said, putting out his arm to hold Angela back. "Why hasn't he struck me as the bunker-owning type before?"

"He?" I asked, wondering just who Mark thought the owner of Vermillion was. I paused three steps up, thinking fast. "Are you involved in human trafficking?" I asked. His silence answered me. "I didn't think so. Trust me, you don't know the owner like I do," I said, and finished running up the stairs before he could ask anything else.

Paco followed me. "How much of a lead do you need?" he asked quietly when I reached the kitchen.

"Ten or fifteen—thanks," I said, keys in hand, running for my car.

I pulled into Vermillion's parking lot and took up two spaces near the front, running out and up to the front door, only to be greeted by Tamo again, sitting on a high stool behind the hostess's podium, looking even more monstrous in an impeccably tailored suit.

"Bouncing?" I asked him.

"Why not?" He gave me a wide and evil grin.

I did my best to look non-plussed. "Where's Rosalie?"

"In back. Why?"

"Business," I said, and sidled past. The club's music hit me like a fist—it was late, anyone still here and partying needed its artificial drum to stay awake and spending. I swiveled my head and saw Rosalie parting through the small crowd that remained, like a dark wave.

"Tamo said you were here alone?" she said.

"Yeah." I frowned, and looked behind myself, where Tamo had been obscured by a turn in the club's architecture—and for the first time realized the entryway had been converted into a defensible bottleneck after the latest remodel. "Telepathy?" I wouldn't put any creepy power past Rosalie.

"Radio technology. You might have heard of it?" She laughed and then sobered. "Why are you here, Jack?"

"My friend's interested in the bunker option."

"Oh?" Her eyes lit up with the promise of cash. "Well, where are they?"

"On their way here, shortly. I just wanted to set some ground rules with you, first."

"Really?" she said, her tone somehow managing to capture the complete disdain she had for me.

"Yeah. Is there somewhere we can talk?"

Her lips lifted into a smile showing teeth that were, for the moment, human. "Of course."

Rosalie led the way back to her private room. I realized it halfway there, far too late to complain, and I didn't want to seem weak besides. But my gait stiffened, my hands curled into fists, and while she walked across her room to lounge in a chair behind her vanity I stood near the door, for all the good it'd do me.

"Jack, please."

"You're the one that told me that being a vampire meant having a long memory." This room was where she'd changed me.

"Are we reminiscing or are we doing business?" She gestured toward her couch. It was black now, presumably part of her remodel, so not even the same couch I remembered. I grit my teeth and sat down on it, for Angela's sake. "So—the Fleur?"

"Yeah."

She clacked her nails on her vanity in excitement. "Tell me more."

"I can't. I don't know everything, yet."

"Then why're you here?"

"Because I want to make sure you play fairly."

"Jack, if I'd wanted a club at every casino in this city I could have one, easily. You're not the only one with contacts—everyone in Vegas walks through my doors eventually."

"Then why don't you?"

"Because what's better than having business arrangements is having someone *owe* you. And finding reasons to have people owe you is harder than you'd think."

I knew all about how Rosalie liked to be owed. "In case they find out your secret. So they won't hurt you—or tell."

"Precisely. So I'll play fair—mostly—never fear." There was a knock at her door. She went to answer it and stepped outside, returning not that long after. "Sorry, club business. Now—about what your friend requires...."

"The bunker—immediately."

She settled herself regally back into her chair. "It won't be ready until tomorrow night."

"Why?"

"Surely you realize this is short notice, Jack. We use it for storage."

"Of what?"

"You don't want to know. But—what're your next steps? This is related to your werewolf problem, right?"

"Yes." I was still reluctant to tell her anything, but Angela herself would be talking to her shortly. My phone buzzed in my pocket—likely Paco telling me they were leaving. "My friend—she's were. As is her boy. And the Pack can track her. What can you do about that?"

Her eyes glazed in thought. "Difficult—but not insurmountable. I have a magician friend who can help. It'll cost more, of course."

"Of course," I snorted.

"But," she said, drawing the word out. "How long will they need to stay there? Hiding them is not the same as fixing their problem. Why does the Pack even want them?"

"I don't know, yet." I wished I'd gotten a few more minutes alone with Angela in Mark's wine cellar. I still hadn't managed to figure out how Bella and her unborn child had fit in. Except maybe.... "The Pack wants what's theirs?" I guessed.

"The boy?" She considered this. "Werewolves are a slow breeding race—and not for lack of trying, I hear. But why on earth would he be special?" Her eyes narrowed. "Who's his father?"

"Gray."

"Their imprisoned packleader?" She rocked back in her chair and cursed.

"She just needs to buy some time—to figure out a plan to get away."

"Time isn't going to fix this—it's a fight for succession, Jack. Legitimate male heirs—ones born, not bitten—are rare."

I rocked back on my heels. "So? If your magician can stop them from being able to trace her, she can go to ground."

"They won't stop looking."

"The world's a big place. Besides—what other choice do they have?"

KEEP READING

BLOOD BY MOONLIGHT: DARK INK TATTOO BOOK FOUR

AND BE SURE TO JOIN CASSIE'S MAILING LIST FOR SECRET SCENES, MORE CHARACTER ART, MERCHANDISE, AND EXTRA STORIES!

DARK INK TATTOO SERIES

Don't miss the rest of the Dark Ink Tattoo Series.

...WITH MORE TO COME!

ALSO BY CASSIE ALEXANDER

CHECK OUT CASSIEALEXANDER.COM FOR CONTENT/TRIGGER WARNINGS.

THE DARK INK TATTOO SERIES

Blood of the Pack

Blood at Dusk

Blood at Midnight

Blood at Moonlight

Blood at Dawn

Blood of the Dead *(January 2023)*

The Longest Night (Newsletter Bonus Story & Audio)

EDIE SPENCE SERIES

Nightshifted

Moonshifted

Shapeshifted

Deadshifted

Bloodshifted

TRANSFORMATION TRILOGY *(Coming early 2023)*

Bend Her

Break Her

Make Her

STANDALONE STORIES

AITA?

Her Ex-boyfriend's Werewolf Lover

Her Future Vampire Lover

The House

Rough Ghost Lover

WRITTEN WITH KARA LOCKHARTE

THE PRINCE OF THE OTHER WORLDS SERIES

Dragon Called

Dragon Destined

Dragon Fated

Dragon Mated

Dragons Don't Date (Prequel Short Story)

Bewitched (Newsletter Exclusive Bonus Story)

THE WARDENS OF THE OTHER WORLDS SERIES

Dragon's Captive

Wolf's Princess

Wolf's Rogue *(Coming soon)*

Dragon's Flame *(Coming soon)*

ABOUT THE AUTHOR

Cassie Alexander is a registered nurse and author. She's written numerous paranormal romances, sometimes with her friend Kara Lockharte. She lives in the Bay Area with one husband, two cats, and one million succulents.

SIGN UP FOR CASSIE'S MAILING LIST HERE OR GO TO CASSIEALEXANDER.-COM/NEWSLETTER TO GET FREE BOOKS, BONUS SCENES, EVEN MORE CHARACTER ART, AND CAT PHOTOS!

Printed in Great Britain
by Amazon